A Katrina
Moment

By Alexandra Everist

PublishAmerica
Baltimore

ISBN: 1-60610-017-3
PUBLISHED BY PUBLISHAMERICA, LLLP
www.publishamerica.com
Baltimore

Printed in the United States of America

Dedicated to
Trevor Everist (1973-1993) whose heart was so full of love
that there was no room for prejudice
And
To all the victims who experienced
the wrath of Hurricane Katrina
And
To all the victims of prejudice, both those who are convinced
to believe and those who continue to experience its wrath.

Foreword &
Acknowledgments

The past two years I have spent researching the events of Hurricane Katrina and its aftermath. This book is the result. This story is not about prejudice against any one class or race. It is about global prejudice which may be elicited against any person for any reason, whether it is because of a handicap, ethnic background, race, age, gender or sexual preference. This type of prejudice hates a person for something they cannot change.

New Orleans has a unique culture defined by its diversity. It will rebuild. My fervent prayer is that prejudice will not be involved.

First and foremost I want to thank God for the power and direction in my life even when I did not understand his reasons. There are so many people who were critical to the completion of this work that I could not possibly show my appreciation to them all. Many will go unnamed, people who freely gave of their time as they provided their accounts of what happened. To those I can name I especially want to thank my children and granddaughter who stood by me during the creation of this work, Phaedra and Dion Poppen, Kaitlin Aken, Giles and

Tammy Everist, Grahame and the future Trisha Everist, and Brandon Everist. I also want to acknowledge my parents, Stanley and Maryla Kowalski, who always believed in me and taught me a love for writing. Thanks also need to go to my sister and brother-in-law, Victoria and Perry Chorpenning, who supported me with their unconditional love. I don't want to forget my newly found family, James and Jen Kingsland. My friend, Pat Metlow, continued to remind me that life is a story that needs to be captured, not one that destroys you. I also wish to thank those whose stories inspired me: Darcy with her selfless dedication to her mother and to the memory of Steve who was a true friend to my son. In addition, I want to express my gratitude to all those who were so critical to this book: Sue Hardt and Sherry and Jim Behan. My appreciation also goes to my friends who offered encouragement, Cathy Wichman, Dorothy Nassar, Jackie Edwards, Judy Davis, Sophia McGrew, Katie Edwards, Pat DePalma, Jack Hall, Cathy Brinker, as well as my many friends at Abbott, HealthPlan Holdings, and the alumni of Alliance College. I am also grateful for all my Rotary friends who live their lives without the disease of prejudice: the Libertyville Sunrise Rotary (who without prejudice accepted me as their first woman member), Grapevine Rotary, Port Richey Rotary and Belleaire Bluffs Rotary. I don't wish to forget my church families where God teaches acceptance as a way of life: St. Lawrence, St. Martin's and Calvary. Lastly I wish to thank the passion of my life without which this book would have no beginning and no end.

PROLOGUE

She slowly looked up into his eyes. His love radiated and she knew she would love him, if only for that. She would be forever grateful for what he was giving her. The life she had wanted to live for so long was about to be hers. She tried to focus on the moment. But the feelings inside her began to take control. Slowly the bright blue dissolved into the green eyes of another. Memories began to flood back. The other took control.

CHAPTER 1

His green eyes found hers across the room. All the others around her disappeared from view as his passion swept her off her feet. Few words would be said before she would find herself entangled in his bed sheets. Neither would ever understand what brought them to that place.

Sarah and James met at a singles resort, both desperately seeking something missing in their lives on the last night of both of their respective vacations. They had had other romances in the past. None survived. This new romance was destined to follow the same pattern. This had even more reason to fail. They not only lived in cities thousands of miles apart, they were different.

James' phone calls would begin the next day as Sarah boarded the flight back home.

"Last night was the best night of my life," was the message he left on the phone.

And the calls would continue, sometimes four and five times a day. When he wasn't calling, e-mails filled the space between.

"Why can't I get you out of my head for just a second…the things you do to me," he e-mailed.

Both became intoxicated by the voice of the other. Daily life became consumed by thoughts of the other. There was a call to wake each other up and a call to put each other to sleep. And throughout the day were the e-mails. Each waited anxiously for a response. On the lonely weekends the calls would last far into the night until each fell asleep, fatally clutching their pillows in their arms, laughing about finding feathers in their mouths the next morning.

Chapter 2

Each held important roles in their respective towns. James' restaurant was the hangout for the local New Orleans politicians. His focus on the business faltered. He no longer cared for the contacts he had so carefully cultivated. All that mattered were the calls to his one-night stand. His employees quietly watched his fall, his fall into love.

Sarah found it difficult to concentrate. James' face followed throughout the day. His green eyes found their way into every waking thought. During the day her position at the publishing house kept her busy. But as the clock ticked away towards the five o'clock hour, James consumed her once more. The friends that had once surrounded her life took second place to the calls that would begin once sundown came. The social whirlwind of her previous life transformed into nights spent at home talking on the phone.

And when she finally did fall asleep, her cell phone upon her pillow, restless dreams thwarted any peace. She would find herself wide awake in the middle of the night with unanswered questions tumbling from the far reaches of her mind. Wanting to speak to someone of her indecision but knowing no one would understand. She reached for the notebook beside her bed and wrote the words no one would ever see.

"Oh for the simple days,
The days when sleeping through the night
Was unaffected by memories
Of hands upon my soul
When thoughts of you did not intrude upon my work,
Unaffected by the world without,
Days when loving someone
Did not hurt."

CHAPTER 3

Sarah, ever the more practical one, was well aware that this passionate romance could not possibly survive. The two star-crossed lovers were keeping their lives on hold just for the mere sound of each other's voice. As the weeks turned into months, it became apparent to her that she could only break it off in person. A weekend trip was arranged to a neutral city.

James arrived at the airport first. Carefully clutching the bouquet of yellow roses, he lingered just outside the terminal gates. His anticipation grew as he desperately waited for Sarah to walk through the gates.

Sarah's plane taxied towards the terminal. The flight had been a mixture of anticipation and desperation for her. She so much wanted to see him, but she knew it could not continue. She was determined to stop this before it destroyed both of them. They were much too different. She walked towards the terminal exit petrified of what she was about to do.

Before making it to the doorway, the fear overtook her. She turned around. This was much too scary. Maybe she could find a flight back. She sat down and tried to think logically, something she had not done much of in the last two months. Should she return home and keep up this telephone romance?

Or should she walk through those gates towards her one night stand? She slowly gathered her bags and walked towards her fate.

Their eyes met immediately and it was all over. Magnetized, she was drawn into his arms. All thoughts of resistance disappeared. She fell into his arms as the passion flared. All sensibility disappeared. He exchanged the flowers for the bags she had so recently dropped as they exited the airport.

He looked into her black eyes. "I have missed you so much. I have never felt anything like this before."

"At least tonight there will be no feathers in our mouths," she whispered.

James hailed a cab that ferried them towards a local hotel. In the back seat he clutched her hand tightly in his. He could not wait to have her alone. They walked into the hotel lobby and up to the reception desk. Neither noticed the eyes following them. They were too wrapped up in each other.

As they made their way into the hotel room, shyness overtook Sarah. They had only had one night together. And now a second lay before them. James placed his arms around her, holding her tightly. She shivered. His lips found hers and within moments, her reserve vanished. They fell entwined upon the bed. The moment was all that mattered anymore. They laughed at the thought they would not be clutching their pillows tonight. Their lovemaking reached a crescendo that neither had felt before.

Afterwards they showered together which dissolved into another moment of ecstasy. The passion was uncontrollable. Gathering their clothes from the floor, they dressed once more. James gazed as she carefully did her hair and makeup. He could not take his eyes from her. She was everything he had ever wanted.

They stepped outside the door and made their way to the restaurant next door. Eyes followed but neither noticed. They were too engrossed. They found a corner booth where they ordered a bottle of wine. Other tables came and left as they continued talking for hours. Throughout the meal his hand reached for hers. When the waitress came to ask them if they wanted dessert, they both laughed, knowing there was only one dessert they both wanted. Eventually they realized they were the only ones left. James paid the bill and hand-in-hand they walked back outside. Sarah stopped at a planter just outside the door, and picked up a shell.

Handing it to James, she said, "This is to remember me by."

"I will keep it forever."

Back in their room, they fell once again into each other's arms. The night would provide little sleep for either of them.

The next morning, James woke up first. He gazed down at the face that shared his pillow. Her curls flowed in disarray. Quickly throwing some clothes on, he went downstairs to pick up some coffee for them. Before he left the room, he grabbed the pen and paper from the nightstand.

"Darling:

You looked so sweet, so beautiful lying there, like an angel. I couldn't bear to wake you up. I will be back. I just went down to get us coffee. Thank you so much for last night!

James," he quickly wrote.

Sarah awoke to the sound of his key in the door. Their eyes met as he opened the door. And the coffee would be cold by the time they drank it.

While James took a shower, Sarah noticed the note. Tears came to her eyes. This was not what this weekend was supposed to be about. She had come to break up this long distance romance. They both needed to be with someone more like each of them. She folded the note and placed it in her purse. She would keep it forever.

They decided to walk down to the beach nearby. Sarah went through her bags and found in her haste, she had forgotten to pack her gym shoes. James gave her the ones he had brought. Much too big for her, they were better than the heels she had worn yesterday.

The gulf breeze whipped her black curls across her face, as they walked hand in hand. Both Aquarians, they loved the water equally. They jealously eyed the boats sailing in the wind.

James observed, "How wonderful it would be if we could sail away together and find a deserted island just for us."

At that moment, Sarah wished the same. Life would be wonderful if she could spend the rest of her life with someone who cared as much for her as she did for him.

Knowing the following morning both would be returning home, they decided to order dinner in. They did not want to miss another minute of their time together. They hungrily clutched each other throughout the night. The morning brought tears to both their eyes, not knowing when they might see each other again. Sarah's resolve to break up with him was forgotten.

The taxi brought them back to the airport and James walked her to her gate, kissing her for the last time and not wanting the moment to end. With tears in his eyes, he made it back to wait for his airplane. He pulled out his cell phone and began to leave messages. She would have three from him by the time her plane landed. And he would have three from her by the time his plane reached its destination.

For a few days, their weekend lifted his spirits and he showed a little more interest in the restaurant. But the e-mails were his primary focus. He looked forward to each one that came from Sarah. Even if there was not much to say, it was nice just to hear from her. While picking up groceries, his feet found their way to the card section. One caught his eyes. It mentioned dessert and he knew he had to send it.

CHAPTER 4

Sarah's friends were missing their one time friend. Cathy convinced her to go out with the gang for old time's sake. Although her friends had never met James, they were wary of his attentions. Sarah was loved by everyone and no one wanted to see her hurt.

It was not long before James was calling. Sarah's co-worker, Jack, grabbed the phone from her hands. He questioned James about his intentions. Whatever James said calmed Jack's concerns. He handed the phone back to her, somehow reassured. She never found out what he had said.

Her son, Terrence, also was wary of this man's intentions. He did not want to see his mother hurt. She had been his mother and his father from the time of his father's death. She had been through too much already. He did not want to see her in that much pain again. He and his brothers had spent much time on the telephone worrying about his mother's apparent aberration. This was not the mother he was used to. Terrence was jealous.

CHAPTER 5

The calls continued every day between the two—four and five times a day. James would call as soon as he woke up and together they would fall asleep clutching their respective cell phones to their ears. He begged Sarah to spend another weekend with him. It did not take much to convince her. Her nights continued restless until the predetermined date. Each night would find her waking once more and reaching for the notebook again. In the darkness of the room she would unleash her deepest feelings.

"The fantasy walked through the door
And took me by the hand,
Eyes gazing into mine mesmerized,
The life of ritual took second place
To the interlude
As I became hypnotized in the dance
Haunting music so surreal
Captivating my polonaise
Slowly changing my careful steps
No longer recognizing the movements thus
My feet cavorted in the frantic waltz
As each step became more unknown
Our bodies touched a different zone

The movements raced as the song unleashed
The passion of a thousand songs
Climaxing in a devil dance
Consumed in the fire of desperation
Before withering into silent tracks
As the fantasy retreated
I knew my life had been touched by the spirit world
Never to return to the ritual
Something special, something lost
Forever thankful for the dance."

James was at the airport long before her plane arrived. He wanted to take advantage of every moment of their time together. He waited anxiously for the phone call to tell him she had landed. And he drove around and around past the arrival gate until she finally came through the door. He jumped out of his seat and ran towards her, holding her in his arms and kissing her possessively. He was oblivious to the eyes that watched. She was all that mattered. He reached for her bags and placed them in the back of his Tahoe. And together they got back in.

James clasped her hand possessively in his the entire drive to his home in Marigny. He had difficulty keeping his eyes on the road. He couldn't wait to be alone with Sarah once more.

They finally pulled up in front of his little home. Sarah noticed the grass and bushes needed cutting. She wondered whether his obsession with her kept him from taking care of his place. She knew she was having difficulty focusing on ordinary daily tasks. Inside the door, they were greeted by Agnes, a black lab. She eyed Sarah suspiciously. James was her master.

James placed Sarah's bag in his bedroom, and gave her a quick tour of the place. It was a typical bachelor's pad, sorely in need of care. Sarah's first reaction was to pull up her sleeves and start cleaning the kitchen. There upon the counter under the microwave lay the shell she had given him, safely preserved.

James was not going to allow Sarah to clean. She was here for him alone, not his house. James ordered a pizza for the two of them. She was only here for the weekend and he did not want to waste a moment.

He pulled her down upon the couch, squeezing her so tight she could barely breathe. They sat so close together, there was no room between. She could not feel where he left off and she began. His green eyes stared deep into hers.

"I think I am falling in love with you," he whispered.

Sarah trembled. The words she wanted to hear scared her to death. This was supposed to be an interlude, not something real. She did not answer. She could not answer. She knew she felt the same, but saying the words would make the fantasy go away. Sarah knew her silence was hurting him. Instead she clasped him tighter as she tore at his clothes. She prayed the passion would make up for her silence.

James led her towards the bedroom. Agnes lay firmly entrenched upon the covers. This was her bed and this intruder was not going to take her place. In the end the three slept together, the two on James' side and Agnes still on hers.

Saturday morning, after a night filled with lovemaking, James took Sarah down to his restaurant. He needed to put up some shelves in one of the storage areas and Sarah was more than willing to help. As she entered, his employees observed her warily. Sarah was too much in love to notice. Her face was flushed with happiness as she greeted each employee.

Her friendliness soon chased away the chasm between, except for the manager. Carrie, a cigarette hanging from between her crooked yellow teeth, looked on with derision. She was not happy with this new situation. Carrie worked closely with James and had seen the amount of time he was devoting to this new woman. Until now, Carrie envisioned that one day James might be hers. Hopefully this would only be a temporary interlude. This new woman was so different from what she expected. James had to be crazy to expect this to work.

Sarah looked around at the restaurant that could only exist in New Orleans. Brightly colored mosaic tiles covered the floor. A beautifully embellished tin metal adorned the ceiling. The painted brick walls were covered with vibrant underwater scenes. Even the tables were painted with brilliant fish. An old fashioned wooden mirrored bar stood against the wall. And right next to it hung an old gas lamp. In the back, stood the kitchen behind a woodened windowed wall. Sarah found it altogether engaging.

Together they went to the storage room and spent the next few hours erecting the shelving. After completing the job, they hurried home. They had been around others too long. They needed to be alone once more. Thoughts of an island alone continued to seep into their conversations, somewhere where nothing could intrude upon their need for each other. Again, they ordered in, rather than wasting a moment of their precious time together.

Sunday morning found Sarah guiltily skipping church. She knew she should go, but their moments alone were so few and far between. And she did not know when or if they might occur again. Her plane was due to leave at noon and there was too little time left.

This time Agnes came along for the ride. She jumped into the front seat, her usual position in the Tahoe and turned her back to the door. If she couldn't see the interloper, then she did not exist. James tried to push Agnes into the back seat. She stood her ground. This was her seat. Sarah laughed as James took Agnes by the collar and forced her behind. Sarah jumped up into the front seat and turned to put her hand on the dog's fluffy mane, gently trying to reassure her.

On the solemn drive back to the airport, Jim Croce's voice echoed from the radio, "Time in a Bottle." The two looked at each other and smiled. This was about them. They both relished their time together. They both wanted to capture these moments and savor them forever, saving them for the time when they would no longer be together.

Tears were in both their eyes as James left Sarah at the departure gate. She was everything he wanted. He knew this was crazy, but he had never felt like this before. He was sure she loved him too, but he wanted desperately to hear her say the words. Melancholy overcame him as he returned to his lonely home.

He left two messages before her plane landed and then waited for her to return his call. He waited for the moment her plane would land for her phone. It did not ring. He paced around the room, getting more and more anxious. He turned on the television, in case something had happened. It was an hour past the time she should have landed and she still had not called. He could not help but call once more. This time Sarah answered.

When Terrence had picked her up at the airport, he wanted to share everything that had happened that weekend with her. She could not disregard her son to return a call to the man she had just spent the weekend with. Her son still needed her. So she listened attentively to all Terrence needed to say. Thus she did not immediately call James when she landed.

James questioned why she had not called. She tried to make an excuse but she knew he was hurt. She knew he wanted to hear her say she loved him. She knew she did love him, but she was still too scared. But she now also knew she had hurt him by not calling immediately.

She took the cell phone into her back garden and sat by the pool. No one would be able to hear her here. She whispered into the phone. "James, I do love you."

This was all he needed to hear. The fact she had not called him immediately was forgotten. She was now his.

That night found Sarah reaching for the notebook which held all the feelings she could not keep inside and yet she could not allow anyone to know.

"Life rescinded at that moment
Lost in some adultered state
Living tantalized by a touch
Loving mesmerized by a look
The "L" word had been spoken.

Now that the word was spoken aloud, James became an addict to it. He would not hang up the phone until he heard the words fall from her lips.

Sarah still knew this interlude had to end. It was a moment in time that had to conclude. And in his heart, so did James.

"You are my angel. I hope you find someone first, because I could never hurt you," he pledged. "It has to be you first. I would rather be the one hurt."

CHAPTER 6

In the weeks preceding Christmas, Sarah carefully made plans for the holiday. Terrence quietly observed her preparations and realized the plans were for James. Sarah had always made a big deal of Christmas as he had grown up. But this Christmas was different.

Sarah was determined to make this Christmas something James would remember long after she was gone. Sarah had carefully wrapped 12 tiny presents for each of the eleven days preceding Christmas and each day she would go to the post office to mail one a day to her lover.

The day James received the first, he had spent a difficult day at work. His father was constantly questioning his finances and this day had been no different. In all honesty, his father had every right. He had fronted James the money for this venture. And James was too wrapped up in this new love affair to properly attend to the business. The workers were well aware of this and took advantage of the situation, the bartenders especially.

James needed to get away from this place. He wanted to spend the holiday with Sarah. Finding the package in his mailbox, he quickly opened it. Inside was a short note, stating "Here is dessert until we can enjoy dessert together." Within the box was a small box of Godiva chocolates. He took out one piece and savored the sweetness as it melted in his mouth. His mouth longed for the feel of her lips. The day disappeared. He thought only of her.

James reached for his phone. He had to hear her voice. She was an obsession. He knew he had to see her. He was determined. His first call was not to her. It was to the travel agent. When he did call her, it was to tell her he would spend the Christmas week with her in Dallas. She could not think of any better present he could have given her.

His next call that evening would be to his parents to let them know he would not be at their home this Christmas. This did not sit well with them. Christmas was a time for social gathering and increasing business contacts, not a time for indulging in a transient love affair. They had heard about Sarah, and were wary. She was not a New Orleans debutante and they knew nothing of her family. This would not be good for their reputation; besides, there were a number of well-to-do daughters that would fit their needs. Although they had never met her, they were sure Sarah did not belong in their society.

His family was not particularly religious. In fact, James never remembered his mother even attending church until the last few years. His father never went. The gentile contacts at the Cathedral elevated her social standing. Christmas was for social gatherings with the New Orleans elite.

The next day James found another package containing little bottles of liqueurs "to hold our memories". Thoughts of the Jim Croce song entered his mind. Another day saw a set of multicolored shot glasses, "to toast our moments together." For the next nine days, James couldn't wait to get home to find what surprise would await him in his mail. It filled the minutes until he could once again lie in Sarah's arms.

He drove out to the store and found another card and mailed it off right away.

CHAPTER 7

James arrived at the airport Christmas Eve and flew into her waiting car. His hands, his lips, reached for her and he could not keep them off her. His loins ached with his need for her. Sarah ferried him towards her little home. They walked past her carefully landscaped lawn and through the doorway. She took pride in her home having spent much time remodeling it until it conformed to her satisfaction. Her youngest son and his girlfriend sat in the family room, anxious to meet this interloper who consumed so much of Sarah's time.

This Christmas Eve would not be spent around a dinner table in Sarah's home. This meal would be served in a restaurant. Terrence missed the ritual. Every other Christmas had involved a trip back to his grandparents' home. This was not what he wanted.

Terrence and Julie, his girlfriend, followed Sarah and James into the restaurant. A waiter showed them to their table. The food was traditional American. Terrence missed the ethnicity of his previous Christmas meals.

As the four made small talk, it was apparent the night belonged to Sarah and James. Their eyes burrowed into each other, as they held back the words they wished to say. It was nearly ten by the time the meal was over. Terrence could not wait to get back home. The four entered the doorway and found their places by the Christmas tree. Sarah stood by the bar and poured four glasses of champagne. Too enamored by the moment, she remained oblivious to the distress she was causing her son as she handed each glass out.

The Christmas tree exploded with lights, some dancing and others flickering. At least she retained this memento of Christmas past. Beneath the tree lay piles of brightly colored packages carefully labeled for each of Sarah's sons, as well as for James.

Sarah knelt beneath the tree and selected a gift for each of the others in the room. The rest would remain unopened until the next day when the rest of the boys and their families arrived. After disbursing the gifts, James reached into his pocket and removed his gift for Sarah. The tiny box sent shivers through her. She knew she wanted this but the thought scared her. She carefully unwrapped the package and her eyes glistened with tears. The deep blood red ruby and diamond ring sparkled in the reflection of the Christmas tree lights. Terrence would not remember the gifts he received that night or even the gifts he gave, but he would remember the ring that took his mother away.

Sarah handed one of her many gifts to James. Inside he found the digital camera he had been eyeing. He immediately began to take pictures of Sarah, embarrassing her in front of her son. He turned on the sports setting, not wishing to miss a moment of her.

CHAPTER 8

Terrence watched the two climb the stairs together with resentment. After driving Julie home, he went to his room but he could not sleep. He paced restlessly across his bedroom floor before returning downstairs to stare blankly at the TV screen.

Sarah woke early as she did every day and crept quietly downstairs. In the kitchen she prepared the morning's coffee. She was surprised to find Terrence fast asleep on the couch. She moved about silently so as not to disturb him.

Back in her room, James rustled between the covers. His eyes lit up as he saw her walk through the door. His arms reached for her as she melted once more within his embrace. Their first Christmas morning would not be one either would forget. The passion flared again once more.

"I want you more than I have ever wanted anything in my life," he mouthed into her ear.

Sarah looked down at the ring upon her hand, with tears glistening in her eyes. The strength of his love overpowered her. She had never felt anything like this before.

She could not forget church, no matter how much James protested. Christmas was to celebrate the birth of Jesus. She promised to return soon. In her mind James was a gift from God and she knew she had much to thank God for. This Christmas morning she could not let anything interfere with her resolve to attend church, although she did end up going to the later service.

Sarah always listened closely to the minister's sermons. Somehow his message seemed to touch that part of her soul where little else could. That Christmas sermon made an impact more than most. The pastor spoke of the temporary nature of Christmas gifts. And he told of all the gifts God gave us on earth, also temporary. The only eternal gift was that of Jesus and God's love. She realized what she had found in James was just that, a temporary gift, something that one day would disappear. Even so, she knew she would be forever grateful for this gift, even long after it was gone.

While Sarah was gone, James wrapped the blue and white robe Sarah had also given him the night before around his body and made his way downstairs to the kitchen. Terrence still lay upon the sofa. He awoke to find James pouring himself a cup of coffee. He eyed James suspiciously. He did not like this man's familiarity. This was his kitchen. And he was in a robe. This was not his home. Terrence wanted him gone.

When Sarah returned she found James at the kitchen table sipping coffee with Terrence and Julie. She found comfort in the familial atmosphere. She was unaware of the resentment that filled the air. James was not used to sharing her and neither was Terrence.

When the other boys arrived, they were also wary of what they were seeing. This was not the mother they knew. She was definitely not acting like herself. The family sat around the Christmas table, each son silently wondering what this all meant. In the end, they all agreed the glow in her face was enough for them to let her be. They had not seen her that happy in a very long time.

CHAPTER 9

James flight was due to leave early New Years Day. New Year's Eve was never a good day for Sarah. It was the night she had lost her husband during a freak ice storm in Dallas. The roads had been caked with ice that night as he raced back to spend the evening with his family. Sarah would remember very little of that night—the phone call, the hospital, and the shock of his death. And the long lines at the funeral. It had been surreal—as were the months and years that followed. This was not the way she had planned on raising her family. But there were no options. There were dates, there were marriage offers, but her children came first and none of the men she met were right for raising her boys. She would not trust her children to anyone.

Needless to say, Sarah hated New Year's Eve. The memory of that night haunted her. She became determined to make this New Year's Eve different, one that she could remember with happiness. And she was determined that their last night together would be one James would never forget. She made reservations at a local hotel. They spent the evening having a slow romantic dinner. Sarah stared at the ring upon her hand throughout the meal. This all felt so right, and yet so wrong.

As midnight approached, Sarah led James towards the

elevator. No one would be using the elevator at this point of the night. They pushed the button for the 12th floor and as the elevator rose she reached for James zipper and lifted her dress. He was excited before she even began. His lips locked upon hers as he leaned her back against the wall. They both realized the elevator was stopping at a different floor. Quickly they rearranged themselves as the door opened to a group of teenagers. The two reconsidered their options. This time Sarah led James to a deserted stairway and there they completed a new New Year's memory.

CHAPTER 10

New Years Day found Sarah driving to the airport to drop James off. He slept the entire flight home. The week had been exhausting. And he knew he would have to go straight to his parent's house in the Garden District as soon as he landed. They were not happy with him. They distrusted his involvement with someone whose family they knew nothing about. He withheld much from his conversations with them, answering their questions with short phrases. Sarah was his alone and he would not let them intrude. They may have controlled his life but he would not let them control his love.

He assuaged their anger by promising to travel to Michigan in January for his great-aunt's 90th birthday. His parents and his brother's family would all be going to his grandmother's farm in Michigan. James knew it was not the best time to be away from his business, but the family insisted and their command was law. He called Sarah to complain. She was the only one that understood how he felt. He was surprised to find she would be attending a convention in Chicago that weekend. He could not believe his luck, another chance for a rendezvous.

He had to find an excuse to get to Chicago while he was there. Lying to his family was not an issue. It had been a much too commonplace ritual from the time he was young. It was inherent in his family. Everyone lied to keep up the social pretense.

James booked his flight into Chicago just to have an excuse to see Sarah. He rented a car and started out upon the snowy highway towards the farm. Growing up in the South, snow was an adventure. He called to tell Sarah he took out the maximum insurance on the car, just so he could have fun in the snow. He wanted to speed upon the icy roads and perform donuts. She warned him not to, but James was reckless like that. Nothing would change his resolve to make a drive upon the icy roads an adventure.

James drove up the long driveway, peppered with antique lampposts. Built in the 1800's, it resembled an antique museum with wrought iron furniture assembled in formation on the patio in front of the door. Snow blanketed the scene, like a Norman Rockwell poster. A long front porch surrounded the home. To the right stood the bunkhouse where James and his brother would sleep.

Stepping in the doorway was like stepping back into the past. The home was filled with artifacts from long ago, not the least of which were his aged relatives. They welcomed James warmly. He did not often attend their gatherings so this was a surprise. Through the door to the right was a sunroom where most of the younger cousins were gathered. To the left was the dining room where the older relatives and his parents sat. They were glad to see that he had made it.

Downstairs James found his brother and his wife playing with their children. The lower level was the most exciting room of the farmhouse. Upon an antique desk sat a copy of the newspaper announcing World War II. In a cabinet stood an old pill-making device that his grandfather had used. A grandfather clock signaled the hours away. The entire room held a feeling of homeliness of another era, homeliness not found in his parent's home.

This weekend was more than just a chance to celebrate a birthday. Each of the family members had gathered to try and stake their claim to the property within the house. A land developer had approached the family to sell the property which included a lake and four outbuildings. No member of the family wanted to be cut out of their piece of the pie. With cameras in hand they went from room to room deciding what each wanted. The women clamored into an upstairs bedroom to divide the grandmother's jewelry.

All James wanted was to get back to Sarah. He didn't want to be part of this rape of his grandmother's land. Whenever he was with his family, he felt so helpless, as though he was a puppet forced to perform at the whim of society. This made him lash out. This made him reckless.

Saturday morning found him acting upon his wild desires. Going out early on the snowy lanes, he sped as though he could speed no more. At that moment he was master of the land. He was master of his life. As the speedometer rose, his sense of power rose. He was in control. The car careened across the snowy lanes and then spun out of control. The car jumped through the air, crash landing in a ditch.

James did not have appropriate clothing for the weather. His jacket, covering the silk teal shirt Sarah had bought him, was made for a winter night in New Orleans not in Michigan. His shoes were gym shoes, and before long they were soaked through. He walked along the snowy road, praying for someone to come to his aid. One of the neighbors saw him walking and went back to get his tractor. The rental car, with only a few hundred miles on it was a disaster. The front fender was badly misshapen. The rim of the tire was bent. By the time most of the family was out of bed, James had already had his adventure. He could afford to put up with them once more.

CHAPTER 11

The afternoon was reserved for the obligatory family chore. Everyone hated this duty, even James. His father routinely stated if I ever get like that, shoot me. It was the visit to his grandmother. As much as the each member of the family wanted their share of his grandmother's belongings, no one wanted a share of her. Placing her in an out-of-the-way nursing home, close to no one, was the only solution. Their communal justification was that she didn't know who they were anyway so why did it matter where she was. No one seemed to realize that it should matter to them because she was their mother. Besides she was an embarrassment. How could they possibly allow her to be seen by society?

James and his parents entered the neatly kept nursing home. It didn't smell like most. It was clean and fresh. The nursing staff doted on the grandmother, who gave them no problems. A tootsie pop would satisfy her every need. The aid wheeled her into the waiting room where the family members sat. At times "Gram" would appear to recognize one of them, but in a different time at a different age. She clicked her jaw after each recollection, symbolically chastising them for not remembering the incidents she spoke about. Each person wanted to run. She was a reminder of what might become of each of them. They did not want to be reminded. As soon as humanly possible, the visit was concluded as everyone happily went out to enjoy a meal at a local restaurant. They had dutifully performed their obligation. They could go on with their life.

The farm was where James and his brother had been sent every summer. The place held a wealth of adventure for two young boys from the South. While his parents spent the summer traveling the globe, James and his brother learned how to live in the North. The days were full of dips in the lake and tractor rides. And adventures not found in the South.

During the rest of the year a black nanny provided his maternal needs, gently making his meals and cleaning up after him. This was no different from any of his friends. He did not know there were families that did not live like his.

The family was divided over the farm. An offer of $5 million had been made and the majority wished to grab and run. The grandchildren somehow felt differently. This is where they had spent every summer, where they had fished and swam, where there were loving arms to hold them, memories of a childhood past.

Chapter 12

James telephoned Sarah at every opportunity when he could get away from the family. Sunday morning could not come soon enough. Blaming an early morning flight, he drove as fast as possible in the damaged vehicle. It no longer careened but limped towards O'Hare. Sarah waited patiently at the car rental lot. He jumped into her waiting car. His shoes were still soaked from the previous day's adventure.

He pressed his lips solidly against hers. This was the moment he waited all weekend for. There was so little time. They found their way to Sarah's hotel room and within moments became enmeshed in the sheets. Ecstasy had returned to their lives.

"I love you so much! I couldn't wait to get here," he said. "It was murder watching everyone fighting over the furniture when all I wanted to do was be with you."

Later, finding an Asian restaurant, they ate, their hands touching throughout the meal. Sarah drove him back to the airport, tears falling once more.

Sarah's restless nights again brought anguished hidden thoughts to paper.

"Knowing our unspoken needs,
God gave us each a temporary gift

One we must return
When our destined paths resume
One that offers solace
In a single space in time
One that consumes us with passions
Deep in the moments that we have left
One that transcends
Understanding to the audience about
One that opens peek holes
To the treasures hidden within
One that will forever
Linger in remembrance dear
Though trembling in fear of the time
When I must return that
Which was never mine
I thankfully accept the coming pain
The future holds in store
Well worth a single moment with the gift."

CHAPTER 13

As each week passed, the need for each other grew. They connived to find excuses to see each other. When Sarah heard of a Publishing convention to be held in New Orleans, Sarah quickly made reservations. She called James. This would be on his territory. She hated their secret life. In everything she had ever done she had felt pride. Now, when she was so happy, she felt ashamed.

Sarah reserved a hotel in the French Quarter. Her flight arrived, and there he waited. She jumped into his car and raced towards her hotel. The doors of the room were barely closed when they tumbled into each other's embrace. Sarah was responsible for setting up for the convention, so she left James still curled up upon the bed. She worked feverishly to fix the tables and slipped back to the room.

She was surprised to find another man there. James introduced Sarah to his brother. The brother's eyes looked at her beaming face and slowly warmed to her. Even so, the small talk remained somewhat tense. The brother made an excuse to leave and all sighed in relief. James and Sarah just wanted to be alone.

Not surprisingly, James parents found out. They summoned his presence that evening to dinner at Toulouse. He was not going to leave Sarah behind. Sarah looked at her wardrobe.

Meeting his family scared her to death. Nothing was right. She tried on each item she had brought and found each lacking. She hated shopping, but knew this was one time when she had no choice. She walked over to the shops on the pier. She tried on dress after dress. Some were too low, others too short, and others too slinky. She finally settled on a black and white sundress, hoping it might make a difference. She somehow hoped it would conceal the difference.

CHAPTER 14

The streets of the French Quarter were crowded with tourists anxious to intrude upon the wild antics of this town. Sarah and James walked hand in hand down the narrow crowded sidewalk. The smell of urine clung in the air. The partygoers took no notice of the couple.

James was very familiar with the area, passing a gentleman's club, as he led her into Toulouse. Toulouse was the meeting room from New Orleans society. Sarah found it fascinating with its eclectic crowd of New Orleans gentry.

Just before they reached the place, James mentioned, "I have something I need to tell you before we go inside."

"Is there something wrong?" Sarah asked quizzically.

"My parents think I don't drink," he replied.

They were at the door, so Sarah had no time to question him about the revelation. He always had a drink whenever they went out.

They entered. All eyes turned to stare.

The red-haired whiskered maitre'd stood at the doorway in a black jacket, white shirt and striped tie. They passed a maroon walled foyer with a walnut framed mirror where each female guest vainly approved of their reflection before entering the dining area. Beneath the mirror stood a long table heaped with daintily folded napkins, keeping the ladies from peering too closely at their wilted reflections.

The maitre'd was the first to recover his composure. Hand outstretched he reached to shake James' hand. Sarah self-consciously cowered behind. The dinner guests all eyed James knowingly. As each customer turned, she squirmed, knowing they found her lacking. She was not one of them.

The two were led to the table where the family waited. James held her seat for her and she shrank into the chair. No one else stood to greet her. She knew this was a mistake. She would never be allowed to be a part of his life. She would never be accepted. They were members of the beautiful people and they did not allow intruders. She couldn't wait for the night to be over.

Sarah shyly looked around the table. The mother, whose carefully coiffed hair held nothing out of place, was donned in an expensive designer outfit. The father, dressed in a suit, spoke quietly, careful not to bring any more attention to the table. No questions were asked of Sarah. She was merely another one of James' aberrations. He was obviously not thinking clearly. Or maybe it was just another act of defiance; another example of his flaunting the family values. The parents would make sure this idiocy would pass.

The waiter came over to the table and took their drink orders. He returned with mixed drinks for everyone except James and Sarah. She would not drink if he could not. Instead they each had soda.

The waiter began to take their dinner orders. Sarah was mystified. She had not seen a menu. She looked at James and whispered her need for a menu. Annoyed, the waiter brought it and handed it to her. Impatiently he waited for her to make up her mind. She was not sure what she chose. She just wanted the embarrassment over.

Realizing she wasn't welcome, Sarah retreated to that island in her mind. She focused her attention on the crowded noisy room. The din of everyone speaking reverberated. She didn't even try to concentrate on the table conversation as voices blended into one another.

The table next to theirs was occupied by six men and women in their 70's. The women all flaunted festive Easter bonnets. The men were each adorned in white dinner jackets and dark shirts, one with a bright red bow tie.

A family sat at the table on the other side. The boy in their midst uncomfortably squirmed as he pulled at the uncomfortable tie around his neck. She watched as he slowly began to slip beneath the table, before a rigid hand pulled him back into the appropriate position.

At the back of the room there stood a stairway leading to an upstairs dining room. Sarah wondered if the atmosphere there might be any different.

All the men in the room wore dinner jackets of grey or black, mostly brought out of mothballs for the occasion. For those who dared to enter this realm without a jacket, a few extras were held in safekeeping at the door. Sarah realized this society was all about appearance. Back home, people wore what they wore to work to go out to eat. Here work clothes left much to be desired, albeit the heat did much to deter appropriate attire.

The waiters, primarily white males with a token woman and minority added for diversity, grouped around each table where a birthday was being celebrated and sang an off-tune chorus. Not one minority customer, though Sarah felt sure there were many in the kitchen cleaning.

She looked down at the white tablecloth and realized with embarrassment that the crusty bread she had eaten had littered the cloth with crumbs, another mark against her.

Round glass water bottles stood upon each table. Silver sugar bowls with packets of sugar. A Cyrillic T embroidered each dinner plate. Upon each table stood bottles of Tabasco and Lee & Perrin's, just like any ordinary restaurant. Why did this one feel so different?

Plate glass mirrors adorned the walls, speckled with black flecks, allowing secret entry into the next table's movements. Sarah looked towards the Exit sign above the door and couldn't wait to get out of this uncomfortable atmosphere. She prayed for a fire drill that would whisk her out of this place. The fans on the ceiling were dead still like the deadness Sarah felt. Stopped in midstream, no wind to move her wings. Dead!

The people in the room, so consumed with themselves, were totally unaware of the anguish destroying her soul. James, in the bosom of his family, did not notice her distress and this hurt even more.

The stilted conversation continued around her with little said to make her feel welcome. Everyone was uncomfortable and wanted the night to end and it did, not a moment too soon. She wanted no dessert tonight. She just wanted to get out of this hideous place.

The family requested James' presence the following day at their home at 10 a.m. in order to go to his uncle's house. James stated he needed to take Sarah back to the airport and wouldn't be able to get there until the afternoon.

"Then take her to the airport earlier. She can wait there for the plane," the mother suggested.

James refused, something he rarely did when it came to his parents.

No check would be brought. The family had had an account here for over a hundred years.

Walking back to the hotel, Sarah burst into tears. She had known from the start this could not work. Why did she even try?

James held her in his arms, as she sobbed herself to sleep. All he wanted was her, but he knew the power his parents wielded. When he was with Sarah, he knew he could stand up to them. But she was only there occasionally. And now that they knew, their power would take control of his life.

CHAPTER 15

Before taking Sarah to the airport, he stopped and bought a dozen yellow roses, handing them lovingly to her before she went through the airport doors. She took them with tears in her eyes.

When she got to her seat, she noticed two other women in the row, one of them with red roses. The one in the middle laughed and said, "What did I do wrong this weekend. No one gave me roses."

Throughout the plane ride Sarah noticed the flowers slowly wilting, both hers and the red roses. She wanted desperately to keep them alive. She requested water from the stewardess and tried to nurse them back to health, but by the time the plane landed, she realized her efforts had been in vain.

She knew James might ask about the flowers. She did not want him to know they died. She briefly considered going out and buying another dozen just like them so that she could tell him they were still beautiful. But then she realized that that would just be lying to him and she couldn't do that. So when he asked, she told him how she had attempted to keep them alive throughout the trip, and how she had thought of buying new flowers. He told her he loved her even more for the attempt. She carefully placed the wilted petals in her day timer, a memory she could keep forever.

Chapter 16

James knew he needed her with him. If she was with him, he knew he could stand up to his parents. He began to beg her constantly to move in with him. But when he started talking of selling his business, Sarah knew she had to make a decision. There were only two choices: end the affair or move in with him. She could not let him give up his business for her. She did not own a business. She had been successful in Dallas. Surely she could get a job in New Orleans.

She carefully wrote out her resignation letter and walked into the office of the CEO. "Absolutely not!" was his response. He refused to accept it. He knew how critical she was to the business. "What are you thinking of? Moving in with some long-distance relationship? What do you know of this man? Has he made you any promises? Is he planning on marrying you?"

Sarah trembled, acknowledging the wisdom of his words. "He has promised to love me forever. I don't need anything else. I love him and he loves me. That is enough."

"Telecommute, until you come to your senses."

Sarah realized this might be the answer she needed. She ran back to her desk and e-mailed James. She was giving him the answer to his wish.

"I miss you so much each day it hurts. All I think about is you. I can't wait for you to be here," was his reply. "I just want to be with you forever."

Sarah never questioned what those words meant.

Sarah would not sell the house. This was her son's home. He would not move with her. His life was in Dallas, not New Orleans. She would leave her home in his capable hands.

Sarah began to make preparations for the move. Sarah rummaged through her closets and carefully packed the things she would need. She gathered her treasured belongings from her house, her pictures, her clothes and her books. That would be all she would need. The rest she would leave for Terrence. Everything else was with James. She put all her trust in him. He was her beginning.

Terrence was appalled at his mother's decision. Was she out of her mind? This man was nothing like her. Terrence did not trust him at all. She was giving up her job, her home, her friends, her family, for what? This man would only bring her down. It was not like James was offering to marry her.

She drove through the night. Nothing could keep her from him. The humid air hit her each time she stopped for gas. Most of the way they spent on their respective cell phones. They never got enough of the sound of each other's voice. It didn't matter if they were only speaking nonsense, as long as they were speaking to each other. When she reached his house, he was waiting anxiously at the window, Agnes as well. They melted into each other's arms.

"At least we are now together forever. That is all that matters," he whispered into her ear. "I have waited all my life just for you."

All her trepidation of whether this was the right thing to do disappeared. She was home.

Helping her move her belongings into the house, he soon realized his bachelor closet would not be big enough for both their clothes. Thoughtfully, he moved his into the back bedroom, so she would have room.

CHAPTER 17

The days took on a familiar feel. Together they began to settle into this life. Each morning would begin the same. Waking up in each others' arms and beginning the day with love. Sarah would make the coffee and serve him in bed. Then, together, they showered in their communal bathroom.

Sarah would find love notes scattered throughout the house, each day something new. They were just short one-liners speaking of his intense love and need for her.

"I want to be with you forever."

During the day, Sarah continued to work for the publishing company. And then in the evening she went over to the restaurant. Business had slumped in the previous year. Sarah knew she could get it back on track.

Often, on afternoons when business was slow, James would rush back home for some "afternoon delight" as he called it. No matter how often, no matter when, ecstasy consumed the two. They could never get their fill of each other.

James' friends, Karen and Larry, called one weekend, to invite them over to go boating. James had been ignoring their invitations since Sarah had arrived. But this time he decided to accept.

This couple, although successful, were not part of society. Neither had finished high school, but had done quite well financially. They owned a successful construction business but had grown up poor, "trailer trash" by his parent's standards.

Sarah dressed in her bikini and glanced in the mirror, wondering whether it showed too much. James loved watching her beautiful body. It turned him on every time. In his eyes, she could never show too much. She quickly covered it with a sundress, not quite sure whether she would remove it. James dressed in his favorite silk teal she had given him. Sarah loved seeing him in it. It brought out a wondrous sparkle in his eyes.

They grabbed Agnes and opened the front door. Agnes ran toward the Tahoe jumping into the front seat once more and turned her back to the door. The dog still thought of this as her seat. James pushed her into the back and Sarah got in.

Karen and Larry welcomed Sarah, James and Agnes with open arms. Together they drove down to the dock and boarded the sailboat. The day was perfect. Fluffy white clouds drifted by in the sky. The men shared beers as Sarah sipped her wine.

Agnes also loved being upon the water. She stood at the helm of the boat jumping in to the inviting water the moment it stopped. She happily splashed through the water, content with the day. And then suddenly she started swimming to shore. James yelled out for her but to no avail.

Sarah dived in to retrieve her. Agnes, seeing Sarah in the water, immediately changed direction. Agnes had become quite fond of this new interloper and obviously thought she was drowning. Agnes was not going to let her new friend down. As she reached Sarah, the dog pounced upon her, pushing Sarah under. Gulping a mouth full of water, for a moment Sarah felt scared.

"Hold on to her collar," yelled James. "She'll drag you back."

Sarah did as commanded and received a welcome ride back to the boat. Getting back onboard, the warm sunshine caressed James' two favorite girls as they both dried off.

Sarah took out the camera to remember the beautiful day. James looked towards her, clouds in the distance, with a smile so radiant she had to capture it forever. His eyes sparkled reflecting the color of his shirt. At that moment life seemed perfect.

Sarah continued taking pictures when suddenly the winds started to increase. The mast of the sail came crashing down upon her shoulder, quickly leaving a massive bruise. The peace of the day had ended. It was time to return to reality. Starting the motor, the friends navigated back to shore.

They drove back to the couple's house and Sarah helped Karen prepare the food for the barbeque as the men happily consumed the last of the beer. Sarah made small talk with Karen. She felt accepted. Maybe this couple had gotten past the difference. Maybe they could be friends.

CHAPTER 18

Sarah sorely missed the companionship of friends. Since they rarely went out, she met no one. She decided, she had to join a group if she were to find companionship.

Sarah found the local Rotary club and soon became immersed in their activities. At least, the members didn't notice the difference. She needed this acceptance in her life. She gladly volunteered to host a charity auction and immediately went to work soliciting donations. She ended up bringing in more than they had ever expected. Always the over-achiever, she would not do less

Each Sunday she went to the local church and slowly made acquaintances. She tried to involve herself in the congregation, volunteering to take over the management of the gift shop. Under her guidance, she turned it into a profitable venture for the church. She inventoried all the old stock and rummaged through the catalogs trying to find articles that might sell.

Looking through the unsold inventory, she found a brass door knocker with the words "Peace to all who enter here." She knew she needed for their door and swiftly purchased it. Making her way home, she found a hammer, and James was awoken to the sounds of hammering at his door.

Now, maybe friends would come.

James quietly put up with her idiosyncrasies, although he never understood why she needed more. Wasn't he enough for her?

CHAPTER 19

On days that James came back early from the restaurant, he expected Sarah to be at his beck and call. She tried to submit to his desires but there were times when work had to take precedence. Her fourth week there, James came back just after lunchtime. She knew immediately, he was upset.

"Now that you have moved in, you are ignoring me. You are holed up in the back bedroom on your computer. Is this how you treated your husband? I thought you came here to be with me."

This was the first time Sarah had heard James wrath directed towards her. She wrapped her arms around him and tried to appease him. She knew she had to put her heart and soul into this relationship. There was only one thing she could do.

Sarah realized she could no longer give her work the time it required. Sadly she wrote her second resignation letter. This time it was accepted with no questions. She sadly acknowledged the end of her career.

Sarah resolved to turn the business around. This was for their future, so she put her heart and soul into it. She started out by reviewing the accountant's records, at least the ones she could find. James's office was in total disarray. Boxes of accounts, vendor contracts and invoices were scattered across the floor in no apparent order. Those accounting reports she did find were filled with discrepancies. She blamed his negligence on herself. She had kept him from his work. Thus began the reversal of the business.

She had to put some organization into the business. She started with the files, buying enough cabinets to organize the mess. Somewhere, during this organization, she realized the only way to get her hands around the disaster was to build James a new office. Under Sarah's hands, a back storage room piled high with clutter was transformed into a working office. On her hands and knees, Sarah knelt and scrubbed the floors and painted the walls as James dealt with the day-to-day operations. She tore out the linoleum and ordered a rich burgundy carpet. Under her careful hands, the room became an office.

She ordered boating pictures for the walls. Their dream of the sea and an island took shape in the office she created. She purchased a ship model and placed it upon a shelf she built. She bought a collage of ship's knots for the walls. She realized James needed a place to hang his jackets, which were typically strewn across his chair.

Going down to the open market, she found a piece of driftwood she knew she could transform. She carefully sanded the piece and then varnished it till it shone. She found some brass hooks made like sailors and she carefully screwed them into the wood. She created a memento filled with the love of her heart.

James had heard grumblings from the employees about their lunchroom facilities. Sarah knew she had to treat them equally. She had three boys. She knew she had to do the same for them. Another month of tearing out flooring and painting walls and moving furniture went by. She chipped away at the old linoleum and it came away in pieces. As she looked down, she observed her hands. The ring James had given her was covered in splotches of paint. Her carefully manicured nails were no longer so. Calluses had formed on the palms of her hands. But she did not complain. What she was doing was for the two of them, for their future.

Each morning she went to the restaurant with James. On days he was missing a waitress, she became one. When he needed a busboy, she became it. When he needed a dishwasher, she became it. She did not notice her life dissolving into oblivion. All she noticed was the love James had for her.

When the restaurant was running smoothly, she delved further into his accounts. She created an accounting program to highlight the anomalies and graphed history and production. She was surprised to find a business plan had never been written. She resolved to correct the situation. All businesses needed a strategy in place.

Somewhere during her investigation, she realized the business really did not belong 100% to James. It was held in his parent's names. He paid a monthly mortgage to them. This surprised her. All the work she was doing for their future was actually going to safeguard their investment. She quickly disregarded her suspicions as pure selfishness.

James watched as she transformed his business. And realized even more how much he loved and needed her.

CHAPTER 20

Each evening James and Sarah went home together, both tired from the physical activity. Some nights they would bring home food from the restaurant. But other nights Sarah insisted on cooking. James would lie upon the couch, half watching her and half watching TV.

Agnes would stand at attention close by her feet as she cooked, diligently waiting for Sarah to drop something she was making, especially if she was making pico de gallo. Sarah was amazed at the dog's affinity for jalapenos. If a bowl of the condiment was accidentally left upon the table, Agnes would gently pick it up by her teeth and ferry it outside where she could savor it to her heart's content. This usually took place the moment James and Sarah began to kiss.

Together they ate off the coffee table in front of the TV. Sarah had always served meals at the dining room table. But this was James' home and she had to conform. And she had always been particular about cleaning up immediately following a meal. But James insisted she sit with him. So she accommodated his wishes.

Of course, this would soon become another performance of lovemaking. Not that this ever bothered her. She could never get enough of his lovemaking. She loved being held in his grasp. At these moments, time stood still. Life belonged to them alone. When James' gaze would move back to the television, Sarah knew it was safe to return to the kitchen.

James and Sarah laughed about never being able to get through a movie without falling into each other's arms. They could only watch DVD's because they always needed to rewind.

Sometimes, on Sunday afternoons James would hitch up his john boat to the back of the Tahoe and drive to the Chalmette boat launch. Agnes was in her element. She sat proudly at the helm, like the captain of a ship. Out in the gulf, James let his inhibitions run wild. He raced the boat over the waves, water streaming over them. When they were far enough away from any other vessels, they would anchor, pull out the lawn chairs on the boat, and bask in the sun. Agnes would jump in the water, happily swimming in circles around the boat. James would place his arms around Sarah and gaze lovingly into her eyes. At these moments they were alone in the world on their own floating island. Life was perfect.

James would pull out the camera Sarah had given him and take hundreds of pictures of Agnes and Sarah. He never felt like he had enough pictures of his two favorite girls. Sarah swore he had taken more pictures of her than the number taken throughout her entire life

CHAPTER 21

Each week James made the obligatory pilgrimage to his parent's home. Sarah tried to find excuses not to attend. But it was inevitable that she finally join James.

Sarah and James pulled up in front of the Garden District home. A wrought iron fence menacingly surrounded the property daring anyone to have the nerve to enter, securely deterring unwanted guests. James walked familiarly though the gate, Sarah following close behind. Approaching the door, Sarah now questioned her sanity. What made her think any member of this society could ever accept her?

James knocked and the door was immediately opened by his mother, wine glass in hand, dressed to perfection. She welcomed James with a hug, but gave little notice to Sarah. She quickly closed the door behind the two, hoping the neighbors had not observed.

The mother led the two through the kitchen into the dining area. The house was carefully decorated with a collection of antiques. Sarah looked around and found it enchanting. The walls held works of art, but one particularly haunted Sarah. She focused her attention on the painting of a cemetery flanked by a massive old tree. Something disturbed her deeply by the view, but she did not know why.

James' brother and his family had also been invited. Sarah observed the camaraderie that existed between the brother's wife and the mother, both locked in a secret pact against the intruder.

A meal was served in the formal dining room, wine glasses carefully set at each position other than for James. Through the archway Sarah observed the painting peering at her. She quickly looked away. Around the table each member of the family joined in the conversation. No questions were asked of Sarah. No responses were needed.

The talk revolved around the business and its financial status. James provided a copy of the business plan Sarah had written to his father who briefly perused it, before placing it down. He could see Sarah's hand upon it. He was concerned by her influence.

Then the conversation turned to James as a child. "The Devil Child" his mother called him. Sarah turned to look James' face as his mother spoke the words. She saw no impact. Obviously he had heard it before. Sarah wondered at how a mother could say those words. Before James, her life had been her sons. No matter what any might have done, she could not imagine referring to them like that.

The mother laughed about the time James had tried to get into the jar of cookies in the middle of the night. Apparently it became such a ritual, that the family locked the door to the kitchen. James had climbed upon a chair with a screwdriver to unclasp the latch. As he lost his balance the screwdriver became lodged in his cheek. He ran to his parent's room for help, but was told to return to his room. It was what he deserved. Sarah listened in horror. That cleared up the mystery of the lone dimple upon his cheek.

James had often commented on his mother's prowess as a cook. And of that Sarah could not question. The meal was exceptional. At the end Sarah offered to help clean up. The mother and sister-in-law were adamant they did not need her help. So she joined the men in the sunroom. Again, she was merely an interloper upon their conversations.

Her mind drifted to the garden outside. This was without a doubt the Garden District. The yard held a myriad of flowers of all types in colorful bloom, a botanic garden cultivated for the rich. Sarah guiltily wished she could go outside and sit alone among the roses. The beauty of the surroundings was in sharp contrast to the darkness inside. The picture on the wall continued to haunt her. When the women returned, Sarah and James offered their thanks and made their way back to the safety of their home.

CHAPTER 22

James often spoke of a friend named Harry who owned a bar in the Quarter. Every few days James would slip out to visit him. James never asked Sarah to come. She was okay with that. It was only during the day and never more than half an hour. She realized men need some time for male bonding. James never went anywhere without her, so she never inquired about these visits. And she never questioned why she never met this illusive man.

One day she came in the office to find a note from Harry to James:

"What the hell do you think you are doing, you fucking stupid asshole."

Carrie came in the office just as Sarah was staring at the note.

"What is this all about? Have they had an argument about something?" she questioned.

Carrie spoke. "No, Harry just found out about you moving in."

Sarah stood dumbfounded. They had been living together for months now. Why had James kept her hidden? But in her heart she knew. The pain of the difference could not be escaped. She put the note down and pretended it did not exist. She never mentioned it to James.

CHAPTER 23

James's cousin was to be married in June in Florida. The mother's side of the family would be in full force, with the minor exception of "Gram". They would not want her coming and disturbing the event. James and Sarah made plans to go.

Sarah carefully went out and shopped for the appropriate gift. She went carefully through the bridal registry hoping to find just the right gift and just the right card. She carefully wrapped it, hoping to make the right impression on these people she had never met.

As they drove along the dusty Florida highway, love bugs splattered across the windshield. Bugs mortally attached to each other clung together in a death grip. Sarah and James laughed at the similarity of their situation. They held each other's hand tighter wondering if they too were racing towards the end.

Sarah had printed the directions from Mapquest as she tried to navigate towards the town. She never questioned the directions. But somehow they ended up lost. Actually, this happened quite often when Sarah drove anywhere. Her children would laugh each time she got lost on one of these "adventures", as she called them.

James was not amused. He liked to get places fast. He raced along the unfamiliar roads, annoyed that time was wasting. He tried to control his temper each time she called it an "adventure".

"Why didn't you print out directions from one of the other sites?" he questioned.

"I am so sorry, darling," she apologized as she gently placed her hand on his. The touch of her hand immediately calmed him as they made their way back to the appointed road. She resolved not to use the word "adventure" again.

CHAPTER 24

The parents had made the arrangements for the accommodations. They had rented a bungalow for the family. Sarah and James were the first to arrive. Walking through the unfamiliar rooms, they chose what they thought was the smaller, not investigating any further. Exhausted from the travel, they quickly showered together before passionately collapsing upon the bed. They arose and dressed just moments before the parents arrived.

A row of rented bungalows held members of all the family. The mother soon disappeared to visit with her other relatives. James and Sarah sat with the father, a glass of scotch in his hand. He grilled James on the business, and Sarah could hear the desperation rising in James' voice.

As soon as his mother returned, James whispered to Sarah: "We've got to get out of here. I need a drink."

Outside they met a cousin who actually seemed to accept Sarah. Together they found a bar down the road and together they drank way more than they should. Family gatherings apparently had a way of doing that to the members of this family. The cousins reminisced about the trials of growing up in this family, each having been considered the respective "black sheep." The three ambled their way back to the rented premises luckily finding the inhabitants fast asleep.

The cousin had forgotten her keys so she spent the night in the room with James and Sarah. The next morning they were awoken to the uproar of the missing cousin. And at that point Sarah also found they had chosen the wrong room to sleep in. The one they had chosen was supposed to be for the parents. The mother was not amused.

James and Sarah attempted to assuage the anger by bringing home a lunch of barbecued ribs for the family. Sarah carefully chose some salads and desserts from the local delicatessen. They brought the gifts and placed them upon the kitchen table in front of the mother. The mother stood up, stating she had made plans to eat with her sister's family, and left.

The wedding, held in a park-like, sat on the banks of a lake. Sarah loved the beauty of the setting but missed the sanctity of a church wedding. She felt the absence of God in the ritual and wondered at the permanence of such a union. Then quickly admonished herself. Nothing was permanent!

At the end of the ceremony, the family gathered together for pictures. Sarah held back, not wanting to intrude upon the event. James forcefully pulled her into the pictorial memory. She immediately saw the resentment in the family's eyes.

At the reception, no place was available with the family for her and James. She regretted that James had made her to come. He should have come alone, but he had been adamant she join him.

The mother, in particular, seemed angry that he had brought her. In fact, the few times Sarah and James would move in his mother's direction, the woman quickly stood up and left the area.

Sarah noticed another interloper at the bar, the girlfriend of the father of the bride. She had not been included in the family pictures. The two girlfriends, shunned by the family, stood at the bar and drank the night away with only James at their side, drinking surreptitiously from her glass. Although he drank at home, it was never with the abandon he now seemed to express. He continually requested that she refill his "Coke" with another shot from the bar.

The next morning could not come soon enough for Sarah. Both wanted to be back alone, back in the home they had fashioned into their own island. The mother was not to be found when they said their goodbyes.

CHAPTER 25

On the long drive home, Sarah whispered, "Maybe if we had a child, your family might accept me."

"I have never thought of having children before, but I would love to have a child with you," he replied."I can't think of anything more wonderful than having a child with you."

Sarah made an appointment with a doctor the very next day. The doctor assured her there was no reason why she should not conceive.

Together their nights took on a different sort of frenzy, a frenzy of conception. But as the months passed, Sarah began to realize they must look at other alternatives.

"James, maybe it is me. Maybe we should try in vitro fertilization? We could use your sperm and donor eggs so that I can conceive."

"No," he was adamant. "I only want your child, no one else's. If I can't have your child, I don't want one at all."

And so the subject died.

CHAPTER 26

The day arrived when the sale of the family farm was due to close. Now the family converged on the farm. It wasn't like they needed money. It was that they never felt they had enough.

The father would often comment, "If you can't be rich, at least have rich friends." Sarah wondered what was lacking which caused this desperate need to be a part of social gentry.

When the land deal was made, the various facets of the family made plans to deplete the farm of its antiquities; each member frantic to safeguard what he felt was his birthright. The desires of each child and grandchild achieved precedence as each tried to secure their piece of the pie.

Together they drove up to the farm. The family was not happy that he had brought her to their farm.

And together, hand in hand, they walked through each of the rooms and down into the basement. In a darkened corner lay the remnants of a bug infested bearskin rug.

"I remember this from when we were children. I used to lie on it in front of the fire."

Sarah shuddered. It didn't look very inviting to her. James carefully picked it up, like a precious piece of tapestry, something containing a hint of a happier time. He carried it past the family members engrossed in capturing their piece of the pie.

His mother looked at him aghast. This was typical of him, treasuring something no one else could want. In the kitchen, James found a pair of scissors and went outside to cut away the infection that was threatening to overtake this work of art. He knew exactly where he would put it, right above the entertainment center.

The two then found their way into the dilapidated barn. Tucked into another darkened corner, stood the remnants of a broken spinning wheel, a couple of mildewed washboards lying beside it. Sarah knew she could repair and bring both back to life. She could even visualize the washboards shined and varnished hanging upon the office walls.

When James asked what she wanted, she knew exactly what to say. She also knew no one else would want things that needed work. In this world beauty was something only visible on the outside. Even though she knew she had no right to any of it, she also asked for the newspaper announcing WWII sitting on the desk. This she would not get.

The family was shocked that he was even thinking of giving something to her. It is not that they wanted the items. It was just that she didn't have the right to it. She was not one of them.

CHAPTER 27

The obligatory visit was made. Sarah walked behind the family into the visiting room where a frail woman in a wheel chair sat. As the family took their places in front, Sarah sat on a chair to the side. James' mother began to speak to the grandmother. The grandmother stared at her in silence. "Gram" suddenly gazed at James and called him by name. She wanted to know what he had been doing. He answered, torn between his parents' attitudes and his own.

Then the grandmother turned to Sarah. "I didn't see you there. I've been waiting for you. No one does my hair like you do."

For a moment Sarah sat mystified. Then found her speech. "I'll be back as soon as you need me." Sarah was the ultimate servant, something the aristocracy would never know.

Once the farm was sold, there would be no reason to visit the grandmother. "Gram" didn't know them anyway, so what difference did it make. They still knew her, but she was an embarrassment. She wet her pants. Sarah shivered. She hoped that when she no longer knew who anyone was, they would at least remember her.

The farm was handed over to developers, dissolving all trace of the past.

CHAPTER 28

On the long drive home, Sarah remembered her friend Darcy. Darcy's mother had died at fifty-five, from a form of premature senility caused by Parkinson's. Darcy had never questioned where her mother would spend her last years. Although Darcy and her husband were struggling to raise a young daughter, Darcy did not think twice before bringing her into their home. There was not enough money for a nursing home, although if Darcy had had all the money in the world, placing her mother in a home would not have been an option. Darcy's mother deteriorated four long years. She forgot her children. She forgot her personal needs. She forgot how to speak. Although, Darcy could always get her to complete one nursery rhyme. Sarah would state: "A kiss and a peck" and her mother would reply "and a hug around the neck." Those were the only words spoken during her last two years.

Darcy stood by her. Although she did not remember Darcy, Darcy remembered her, taking care of all her personal needs. Darcy became a mother to her mother.

CHAPTER 29

By mid-July, the restaurant business had turned around. Customers began to flock the tables again. Sarah attended the local Chamber of Commerce meetings promoting the business. It was back on track. The office was organized and the bills were finally paid on time.

One Sunday, the pastor asked Sarah to represent the church at a week-long retreat. She knew this would not sit well with James. But she had always been so active in church. And she knew she should be thankful to God for all she had received. When she said yes, James was not happy. Again she was leaving him for someone else.

He usually didn't mind her going to church on Sundays since she always went to the early service and was always be back before he woke up, but this was different. She belonged to him and he did not want to share.

The retreat was a two hour drive from New Orleans, set out in the woods. The peace and serenity of the surroundings brought back memories of camping out with the boys as children. Sarah missed those times.

James' calls began immediately. "I miss you so much. I can't stand coming home and not finding you here. I can't wait for you to come home. The house is empty without you. Agnes waits at the door for you to come back in."

By Tuesday, he was begging her to meet him for dinner half way between them. "Meet me tomorrow night for dinner."

Sarah found the thought exciting. It was like a date. They rarely went out anymore. She looked at the clothes she brought, nothing appropriate for a "date." She tried a couple of outfits and finally settled on something. Not knowing the area, she soon found herself lost, having another "adventure." She had given herself extra time to find the place, but even so, she was late.

He sat at the table on his second glass of wine when she arrived. He folded his arms around her and kissed her passionately. They were not in New Orleans. They knew no one here. Throughout the meal, he reached for her lips, not wanting to let her go. He begged her to come back home.

"It's only two more days. I'll be back then." She promised.

Friday morning at 5 a.m., she received another call.

"I've been sick all night. And the engineer is due at 9 a.m. to go over the installation of some new equipment. I need you there to meet them," he begged.

Sarah did not realize that James and Harry had actually spent most of the night drinking. Somehow, in their stupor, Agnes had escaped, and the rest of the night had been spent in the search.

Of course, Sarah would never refuse James anything. She knew she had a mandatory meeting at the retreat at 1 p.m. Maybe she could do both. She dressed quickly and sped all the way to New Orleans, praying she would not get a ticket. The engineers waited at the door. She went over the details of the plans, signed the papers, and turned back around to make the return journey. She was exhausted.

CHAPTER 30

James obediently made his weekly visits to the parents. But as the months went by, he began to leave Sarah home more and more. In the beginning, she did not mind it. It was uncomfortable being in the same room with them. But their prejudice began to eat at her. And the day James returned to tell her his mother had arranged for a female to be there when he arrived, Sarah finally lost it. He swore all he wanted was Sarah, and his mother had contrived the meeting.

The woman was a school teacher and he swore he felt absolutely nothing for her. "I only thought of you the whole time we were together. You are the only one I want in my life."

Sarah believed him.

James went over to the liquor cabinet and poured himself a stiff drink. "My mind can't handle this stress and these conflicting feelings...I am at a breaking point. I can't not love you or not love my parents. I feel like I need to disappear to make everyone happy. You can get over me and my family can do anything they want. I want people to be happy for me, not judgmental of social situations. Even the workers are making comments. I want to please everyone and in the process it is tearing me apart. You mean the world to me. I wish love could conquer all."

Sarah wrapped her arms around him, as tears ran down his face.

"In all honesty, I just want to get drunk and go to sleep," he mumbled as he poured himself another.

CHAPTER 31

Somehow, somewhere Sarah realized she had lost herself. She had gone from a highly respected professional to a mother, lover and slave to another, something she would never have imagined possible. She had taken her mother's role. This was not the life she planned. The lovemaking was still incredible, but it did nothing to compensate for all she had given up. She had no money of her own. She had no career.

She was running up her credit card to pay bills. Although, her son was trying to make the mortgage payment for the home in Dallas, there were many months when he just did not have it. And the only place to get it was her credit cards.

James and Sarah never spoke of money. He continued to pay the mortgage and utilities, while she continued to place the groceries and household supplies on her cards. In Sarah's eyes, the business they were building together was for their future. Their money and bills were communal. But this was the first time in her adult life that she had no income. She felt selfish thinking of herself. She had to make a decision. And it would not be easy. She had to return to her career. This did not please James. Why did she need to work? He was giving her everything she needed. The first resume brought a job offer.

She carefully dressed for the first day of work. She had been gone from the corporate world too long. She had begun to question her own knowledge. She drove over the office building and entered the elevator. Nervously, she checked her outfit once more, hoping it was appropriate for the first day. The moment she entered the office, she knew she was going to like this place. Her co-workers, Sherry and Cathy, welcomed her into their midst. Her boss, Sue, called her into her office and handed her the 3 year strategic plan for the business. This was exactly what she was missing. She needed the corporate world. Within the week the four women had become fast friends, laughing over lunch and making plans for the future.

She needed the social network. Since moving to New Orleans, Sarah only had James' workers. They never had anyone over. James was quite happy being with her alone. He shunned social gatherings and the two were becoming reclusive. Whenever Karen and Larry invited them over, James immediately found reasons why they could not attend.

To Sarah he would say, "They are just so uneducated. I am bored when I am with them. Why, they can't even spell. Have you seen Karen's e-mails?"

Sarah reluctantly accepted his decision.

CHAPTER 32

When her workday ended, Sarah would race back home to prepare their evening meal. This was her time with James. Over time he grudgingly got used to her being gone during the days.

"I wish we were back on the same schedule," he complained. "But at least we are together."

Sarah did not forget his business. She continued to review his accounts each night to make sure they did not fall off track again. Weekends would still find her at the restaurant making sure everything was running smoothly, filling in whatever role was needed at the time.

One night after work, he surprised her with four dozen multi-colored roses packed in long boxes. James always knew how to cheer her up. She carefully unwrapped them. But when she opened them, she found to her dismay that they had wilted. She placed them in water, desperately hoping to bring them back to life. She wondered why the flowers he gave her always seemed to die so fast. Was it a reflection of their love? Under her care, the flowers blossomed once more. She lovingly placed them around the house. And when they eventually withered, she placed the last to die in a vase over the entertainment center, a solemn reminder of his undying love and right next to his treasured bearskin rug.

James never understood why she always kept these dead reminders. Or why she kept all his notes and cards he gave her. He had a lifetime to give her more.

CHAPTER 33

By the third week in August, Tropical Storm Katrina began to make the news. By August 25, it was upgraded to hurricane status. It had initially hit southwest Florida as a category 1. As it passed the Keys it was predicted to hit the Florida Panhandle, but later the prediction was changed to the Mississippi/ Louisiana coast. The governor of Louisiana declared a state of emergency, but life in most of New Orleans continued on as normal. This town felt special. Nothing could hurt it. Warnings of evacuation fell on deaf ears.

Sarah and James were no exception. They spent Friday night having dinner at their favorite little French restaurant. James brought out his camera and had the waitress take a picture of them in their favorite corner booth. There was no talk of the hurricane by the wait staff or by the customers. The mood was typical New Orleans.

James' family initially had no plans to evacuate, regardless of the governor's warnings. They had not evacuated during Camille and they were okay. Besides they lived in the Garden district and nothing could hurt them there.

By Saturday evening, Mayor Nagin had ordered a voluntary evacuation, even requesting contra-flow traffic. This did nothing to deter the customers at James' restaurant. In fact it seemed to bring the local customers even more, ready to celebrate a hurricane party. They all had an opinion on the storm, but few felt compelled to leave. They were not going to abandon their homes and businesses. Business was their lifeblood.

Sarah and James returned home that night, drifting off to sleep in each other's arms. Slowly making love, they did not realize that that would be the last night they would sleep in the comfort of their air conditioned home and bed for a long while.

Chapter 34

But at 2 a.m. Sunday morning, their phone was ringing. The parents called James to tell him they were leaving and he should follow suit. James understood their reasoning but believed Sarah and he could ride the storm out. They felt they had to stay for the business. Maybe it was their lack of fear or maybe it was their belief in immortality. James' brother and his family packed up their children with enough clothing and supplies for a couple of days, leaving just enough food for the cat to survive until they returned.

James placed the phone back on the hook and drifted back to sleep, Sarah and Agnes snuggling close beside him, his two favorite girls. By the time they awoke Sunday morning, the Hurricane had reached Category 5 status. Evacuation was now mandatory. Katrina was expected to hit sometime Sunday night.

At noon, the Superdome was opened as a refuge for those who could not find transportation out of the city. James and Sarah began to take the storm seriously. They rounded up the supplies they needed: sleeping bags, batteries, candles and flashlights and prepared to move to the restaurant. Just before piling the supplies into the back of the Tahoe, Sarah ran back for the small Weber grill sitting in the garage. Lastly, Sarah grabbed Agnes and added her to the jumble of items loaded in the car.

Deciding to stock up on batteries and non-perishables, they stopped at the WalMart but found it closed. In fact, most stores were closed. They finally found a small grocery store on Magazine St, but little was left on the shelves.

During the day, the winds picked up as Katrina churned closer. The radio reported water topping the levee. About 2 p.m. the storms began.

James tried to keep in touch with his family through his cell phone. Access, though, was hit or miss. When he could get a hold of them, the family spoke of roads that were totally grid-locked. Traffic was barely moving. James was getting frustrated with the phone service. He had never been very patient, but now almost anything could cause his temper to flare. And not being able to communicate with his parents was adding fuel to the fire. Sarah spoke softly, slowly caressing his hand. His mood remained foul.

Throughout the day Sunday, New Orleans continued the slow exodus. The residents of the towns the travelers passed through were eager to help. The Louisiana plates announced their plight to the world. Strangers offered sanctuary to the many pilgrims.

CHAPTER 35

Sarah and James moved their sleeping bags onto the office floor and prepared to meet the storm. The restaurant held everything they might need, enough food, drink and even more importantly a generator. Plus they had each other. In some odd way they actually looked forward to the onslaught of the storm, somehow stimulating the sense of adventure in each of them.

In fact, a number of customers braved the wind to join them for drinks although most left for the safety of their homes before 8 p.m., much earlier than normal. By then, the talk was only on Katrina. Even these stalwarts began to show fear. When everyone left, the French Quarter became remarkably quiet, like they were the only ones left in New Orleans. Although there was not much rain, the sky was covered with ominous clouds moving frenetically in the sky. Wind chimes from a balcony whispered a song for the coming night. The night air held a strange smell, quite different from the normal pungent French Quarter odor.

Sarah and James retired to the office to try and get some sleep. Their lips found each other immediately and the lovemaking began. They held each other tightly through the night, not from fear but from desire. The wind whipped the outside of the building, sounding like a turbine engine growling outside. The office had no windows, but from inside they could hear debris crashing against the walls. The sounds of glass windows shattered in the streets outside. The lights flickered on and off and eventually the darkness became utter and complete. For most of the night, the walls swayed from left and right. The ceiling fan swayed frantically. The rush of wind could be felt streaming through the floor boards as the pressure outside increased. James went down to open a window in order to relieve the pressure from inside and outside the building. The wind and rain thrust him against the room.

He returned to the office and held Sarah tight. The warmth of their bodies in the tiny office offered sanctuary. Agnes snuggled up closer. Sounds from the outside continued to wake them from their restless sleep. They clung together once more in a sexual frenzy, as they heard the sounds of parts of the upper roof being torn away. And then, they heard water dripping through to the dining room. Together, they went to investigate, but at that point there was little left for them to do other than place pans along the floor. About 6 a.m., the power went out for the last time. And suddenly, without any warning, the winds changed direction.

CHAPTER 36

When the storm finally ended, the streets were covered with debris from miles around. Survivors with dazed appearances appeared through the wind and rain surveying the damage. Even a few cars rolled by, but the normally noisy town was still eerily silent.

The French Quarter appeared to have survived Nature's wrath. The citizens of New Orleans breathed a sigh of relief, thankful that their city did not take the brunt of the attack. That had been reserved for Alabama and Mississippi. But relief would be short-lived.

A battery operated radio was their only means of communication. They turned it on first thing in the morning and the news reports became the background for everything they did. According to its message, Katrina had made its second landfall as a Category 3 at the Mississippi Delta at 6 a.m. By 8 a.m., water was rising on the Industrial Canal. A flash flood order was issued and those remaining were ordered to move to higher ground. The radio reported an 18 ft surge and that the levee was overflowing. As the morning continued, the reports stated the 17th Street Canal had actually been breached. Sarah and James looked at each other in shock. How could this happen? After having survived the fierce winds and storm surge intact, they now faced a sudden deluge.

The effects of the breach were instantly devastating to the residents who had made it through the fierce winds and storm surge only to be taken by surprise by this new factor. By 9 a.m., there were reports of 6 foot of water in the Lower Ninth Ward.

At 10 a.m. Katrina made her third landfall at Pearlington. James' parents had a fishing cabin in Hopedale. It was surely gone. Winds were still blowing about 40-50 mph.

By 11 a.m. there was over 10 foot of water in St. Bernard Parish. Water was rushing into the community with 8 ft surges. Lake Ponchatrain could inundate the city. Any attempts to stop the flow apparently had failed. Besides, pumping would only pump it back into the lake.

Sarah and James kept their minds off the disaster by cleaning. They rolled up their sleeves and began the process. Together they checked out the damage to the roof. Although it has sustained some damage it appeared repairable. The dining floor was covered with pieces of ceiling debris and broken glass. James boarded up the broken windows while Sarah washed and cleaned until the place was almost usable. The power was still not on. Not knowing when it might come back on, they reserved the generator for the food. But water was running and clean and usable, at least for cleaning. It had never been acceptable for drinking. Sarah was always thankful for bottled water.

By now cell phones were completely useless other than for text messaging. Surprising the landline at the bar still worked. But this did not help James in reaching his parents. Luckily Sarah was able to use it to phone her sons to let them know she was okay.

By early afternoon, the winds began to die down and the rain ended. Although it was still overcast, light began to drift through the clouds. Sarah and James walked the streets of the French Quarter surveying the damage. The streets looked like a ticker tape parade of broken glass. The air was hot and still.

They counted their blessings as they passed by another local establishment, the door ripped off and laying in front of it. Amazingly, bottles of liquor stood, lined up like silent sentinels on the back bar, waiting for customers.

CHAPTER 37

By late afternoon they had the business ready to re-open. None of their workers had shown up so Sarah and James felt sure they had evacuated. Other locals soon made their way over to purchase some of the slowly warming beer. The ice was slowly melting in the refrigerator so drinks were served warm in the English style. Sarah and James were surprised to find how many had stayed.

One local told of a mysterious barge that had broken away and had caused the levee breach, something not spoken about on the radio. This would become a common occurrence over the next few weeks, as the only reliable source of information would come by word of mouth.

Another survivor came in to tell of looking outside his door and seeing winds blowing from right to left but trash moving in the opposite direction. Obviously the current was moving faster than the wind. And the water in front of his home was rising by the hour. He complained of a strange pungent smell and a rapid increase in mosquitoes.

Around five o'clock the battery powered alarms began to go off, apparently reaching a critical level all at once, sounding like an air raid warning. The alarms continued until night fell and then went suddenly silent. The air was then filled with a different sound, the sound of croaking frogs in the distance.

James pulled out the barbeque and began to cook steaks, wanting to get rid of the perishables first. Business was brisk as was the drinking. The spirit of the French Quarter was alive and well. Another local pulled out a guitar and the guests joined in singing in off-tune melodies. By the 7 p.m. curfew, the locals crept back to their respective homes, well satisfied by the food and drink.

Outside, was a world of almost perfect darkness, with a few flickering lanterns acknowledging a person's existence. As the humidity increased, the heat of the night became overpowering. The quietness of the night sky was permeated by the sound of helicopters flying overhead. Sarah and James barricaded themselves inside their restaurant refuge. They spent another night safe on the office floor with Agnes at their side. Candles set a mood of romance. They were both feeling no pain from the afternoon of partying. Sarah felt strangely relaxed.

Without any air conditioning, the heat made the office stifling. The humidity inside the room increased by the moment. Dragging their sleeping bags down to the restaurant helped somewhat. They opened the window, hoping to get a modicum of relief from the night air. They softly made love, sweat dripping from their bodies. Then rolled apart. It was too hot to hold each other through the night.

Outside they thought they heard the sounds of gunshots in the distance. They wondered if it might be looters. Sarah and James were sure Agnes's barking would scare any intruders. James had his gun loaded and ready just in case.

CHAPTER 38

Overnight Canal Street did become an actual canal, with whitecaps from the strength of the surge. The downtown streets that had been clear after the storm were filled with a foot or more of ant-filled water, reeking of the smell of gas and oil. Although water lapped at the edge of the French Quarter, it had not entered as if the area held control, an island of sanctuary.

Later that morning, Sarah and James got in the Tahoe to visit their home. Luckily it had withstood the storm remarkably well. The old oak in front of their house had toppled, and was now devoid of leaves. The roof looked like it had some minor damage. And one window was out. Sarah thanked God for having spared them.

Together, they went through the refrigerator, pulling out what they could still salvage and place it in the ice chest. The rest they placed in black garbage bags outside on the sidewalk.

James had heard reports that the Coast Guard had set up rescue operations on the I-10. James was sure they could use his help. Besides he felt like having an adventure. The two hitched up the john boat to the back. After dropping off the food at the restaurant, they trailered the boat over to the Franklin Avenue ramp. There they found others launching boats and a number of survivors sitting under the underpass.

The two quickly went to work to assist in the rescue mission. James started the motor and together they went out in the mucky water looking for survivors. James boated past the submerged houses while Sarah looked from house to house for evidence that someone was inside. Every few moments they would turn off the motor so that they could hear any sounds coming from the homes.

The oil slicks in the drab grey water floated apart and together like embryos in formation. Strangely, they saw no mosquitoes in the water. The oil obviously was a deterrent.

Sarah laughed. "I guess they don't like the smell."

The smell of gasoline was so strong in the air, it began to make her head throb.

Front doors could not be seen, as water lapped at even second floor windows. Blue street signs poked out of the water like eerie channel markers. Furniture, toys and all types of garbage bobbed in the wake of the boat.

Some residents seemed determined not to leave their homes, believing that the waters would recede soon. This was where they lived and where they felt comfortable on their own private islands. One of these individuals actually sat on his roof, playing his guitar and singing. But most were happy to be rescued.

At one house, they found an elderly woman, trapped in her attic unable to get out, yelling for help through a crack in the wall. James grabbed the anchor and climbed to the roof. He smashed the anchor into the shingles again and again and finally made a hole large enough for her to crawl through.

Each time they returned to the launch area, they found more and more people crowded on the ramp. There was no more room under the ramp, so many sat outside in the blazing sun dripping with sweat. James assumed they were waiting for one of the buses to take them to the shelters.

CHAPTER 39

Sarah and James continued their efforts throughout the day till dusk began to fall. Tired and exhausted they drove back to the Quarter. Once inside the doors, they stripped off their muck encrusted clothing and attempted to wash the smell from their bodies.

Locals that had stayed again stopped by. Among those who came was Harry, James' mysterious friend. An aged hippie with grey hair pulled back in a pony tail and his belly showing through the tear in his t-shirt, he did not look the way Sarah had expected. He glanced at Sarah with derision.

He told of his trek to the Central Business District, walking through warm, steamy soup-like water with an overpowering stench. The smell in the air was thick with gas. The surreal reality of the disaster had begun to hit. The storm may have been gone, but what was happening at that point was much more disastrous.

Harry mentioned hearing rumors that the city was going to pump water into the dry French Quarter. No one knew what to believe anymore. The French Quarter survivors stood by waiting for the ominous flooding to begin.

Another resident mentioned hearing reports that gangs had taken over Charity hospital. In fact gangs were attempting to invade most of the hospitals with drugs as the objective. Police had been unable to respond because of the flooding.

Again, according to rumors, Federal troops had been ordered into Charity Hospital to annihilate and dispose of the intruders. There were so many rumors no one knew what to believe.

The number of stalwarts still in town was beginning to dwindle as some evacuated to safer locales. The disheveled group that formed that evening was beginning to show the wear of survival. Although they thankfully looked forward to the steaks that James was grilling. They still had generator power to keep the food refrigerator going, but it was only a matter of time till that ran out.

Luckily, the French Quarter still had running water which was clean and usable, at least until a water main broke under City Park. Sarah tried to conserve what water they had left, saving the melting ice water and the buckets of rainwater. They would be needed to flush the toilets in the days to come.

Civil law had begun to break down. The city outside their area was becoming a war zone. Looting was taking place and was becoming more dangerous than the gas soaked puddles and the downed power lines. Even the police were involved in some of the events, breaking into ATM's and taking SUV's from dealerships apparently for official use.

As of Tuesday night over 85% of the city was underwater. The French Quarter had become a veritable island in the middle of a poisonous swamp. Mayor Nagin advised all remaining residents to leave. Sarah and James would not. They were determined to stay and defend their property. They saw no reason to leave. They had survived Katrina and they would survive this.

Wrapped in each other's arms, their bodies oozing sweat, they feverishly made love. The sweat from James' brow dripped into her eyes and upon her matted hair. Their bodies melted into each other. They had gotten used to the smell of their communal sweat. It was nowhere near as bad as the smell outside.

CHAPTER 40

The two woke Wednesday morning to the sound of helicopters and gunshots in the distance. Luckily the French Quarter remained relatively quiet, though looting in the rest of New Orleans was said to be widespread.

The sky was filled with Blackhawks rescuing survivors from rooftops. Evacuation of the Superdome had begun but was curtailed around 9 a.m. when shots were fired at the military helicopter. Although jet fighters and helicopter roamed the skies, no FEMA or National Guard troops were yet to be seen on the ground.

James and Sarah returned to their rescue mission. When they got there they found out the rescues were being suspended because of the shootings. The majority of the people they had picked up on Tuesday had been elderly. They saw no reason not to continue. By the time they brought back their third boatload of survivors, the Coast Guard was back on duty.

Throughout the day, bodies floated past in the acrid water, with skin bursting with gas bubbles, eyes popping out of their faces. In a town where the dead were honored with jazz funeral processions, these grotesque floating processions of bodies highlighted the abomination.

After the horror of the past few days, the two were almost becoming immune to the sight, but not to the stench. That became more and more unbearable. The smell of diesel fumes was even more overpowering than the previous day. Rumors abounded of gators in the water. Even the bugs and lizards had dramatically increased from the previous day.

From their boat, they saw smoke and fires smoldering across the skyline. One fire broke out on Canal St., sending smoke and fumes into the quarter. Since gas lines were turned off, looters were suspected of starting it. Firefighters had made vain attempts to fight it before giving up.

Before it got too dark James and Sarah decided to check on the homes of his parents and brother. The drive took them past utter destruction. Sagging power lines looked like wilted old men unable to hold the wires aloft. Mardi Gras beads lay scattered along the parade routes, shaken loose from the branches which had once held them. Magazine St., all the way up to Touro Hospital, lay ransacked. Tables and chairs had been taken from the restaurants. The Convention Center sprawled with people half dead from the heat. The A&P was completely plundered and the Oakwood Shopping Center was still sending plumes of smoke into the air.

As they reached the Garden District home, they found conditions not nearly as bad as expected. There were numerous downed trees that they had to drive around, but on the whole, the area had survived remarkably well. Going inside, they found there was still running water, although little pressure. They took advantage of the fact, taking a quick shower. Going downstairs once more, Sarah glanced ominously at the painting upon the wall. Was it trying to tell her something?

Then they went to the refrigerator. Without power, everything was beginning to turn. They scooped everything out into black garbage bags and placed them on the street, not knowing when sanitation service would return. Before leaving, they gathered as much water as the Tahoe could hold.

Then they continued over to his brother's home and did the same. Neither house had sustained much damage, missing shingles and some broken windows, but nothing that couldn't be repaired. His brother's cat roamed the house, none the worse for the wear. They cleaned out the litter box and left some food out. His brother would surely be back soon.

James and Sarah made it back to the restaurant just as the sun was going down. Again, the survivors grouped at the restaurant. The generator gave out that night so they gathered the remainder of the meat and grilled it, not knowing when the electric might come back on. Harry and some other locals stopped by to share the last of the cooked food and the warm beer, but all left early.

Later some of the local police knocked upon the front door. They traded additional firearms and supplies for warm drinks. The officers spoke of martial law being declared. It was not safe to leave the premises after dark. And the darkness by that time was so complete, with fewer and fewer people remaining and fewer lanterns to light the darkness.

Sarah and James lay down in the sweltering heat, not only physically exhausted, but also emotionally exhausted by the massive damage they had seen that day. They clung together once more, sweat dripping from their bodies, holding on to each other, frightened of letting each other go. The death and destruction of the outside could not intrude if they were together. They knew they needed each other now more than ever. Agnes lay at their feet, still not fully aware of what had taken place. Their lips found each other in the darkness, but for the first night since Sarah had moved in, they did not make love.

CHAPTER 41

The calm of the night was interrupted in the early hours of the morning by massive explosions at the riverfront, just south of the French Quarter. They hoped this wasn't another example of the anarchy taking place outside the Quarter. They would later find out it was only tanker cars exploding. Their island was still safe.

The days were beginning to take on an eerie but familiar feel. It was a strange new world with streets inhabited by fewer and fewer locals, just military personnel, television crews and relief workers. No power or water made the French Quarter a replica of what it had once been, almost like being transported into the past, except for the whir of the helicopters in the sky, sounding like a continual fan.

The two spent another day in rescue efforts. Each day they went out, there seemed to be more volunteer boats. It was a veritable armada launching each morning. But each day the stench grew steadily worse as the waters receded and a black muck was left. And each day, they would see more floating remnants of bodies.

Finally, the news reported what they had all been waiting for: the 17th St Canal breach was closed. James breathed a sigh of relief. Maybe the world they had known would start to come back.

CHAPTER 42

The Sunday sky was filled with smoke from all the smoldering fires. Of course, this would be another Sunday when Sarah would not attend church. Instead she tried to make a cold breakfast out of spam and beans. Without any running water, they had been relegated to using paper plates and utensils, but even these were running out. So they ate right out of the can.

The two made their way down to their new daily job. Boaters have an unspoken alliance and this was visible in the rescue, everyone willing to do whatever was needed. There were fewer and fewer people left to rescue. They heard there were children still trapped in a school so the entire fleet made their way over. The building was empty, so the volunteers scattered to find others. This lack of communication continued to hinder rescue efforts.

The few people they did come across were reluctant to leave. The inhabitants were determined to protect their underwater property. Sarah realized that no matter how putrid their homes had become it was still something that belonged to them. These last few holdouts were determined to hold on to what they loved at all costs. Sarah somehow identified with the depth of this emotion. At those homes they left MRE's and water.

At many of the homes, dogs quietly stood guard. At these places, they would leave dog food and water, knowing there was nowhere to take the animals for shelter.

When they returned to their sanctuary, they were surprised by sounds of music and laughter outside. A parade was marching past their street. They went outside to investigate. Katrina had not been able to stop the Southern Decadence Parade. A handful of storm survivors had gathered to stroll down the streets of the French Quarter. One of the members of the impromptu parade sported a hand-written t-shirt displaying the message, "I survived hurricane Katrina and all I got was this lousy t-shirt." Sarah laughed, as a string of beads was launched from one of the balconies. Only here in New Orleans could the parade still go on.

Later the local police stopped by once again to tell them to leave. Sarah and James had remained through the worst of it. They adamantly refused. They still had non-perishables and warm beer. And they still had each other. And surely power and water would return soon.

CHAPTER 43

In fact by Monday, there were areas where water was turned back on. And the Central Business District and the Warehouse District even got their power restored. This provided hope that the French Quarter would not be far behind.

Tuesday, the two went down to the launch site but were told the authorities would be taking over the operation. Civilian help would no longer be needed. Sarah and James got back in their truck and decided to find another launch site along with other rescuers who had been turned away. They thought there still might be some survivors in the Lower Ninth Ward. But most of their efforts that day would revolve on feeding animals sitting on vacant porches.

Wednesday morning, Harry stopped by to report that the Army Corps of Engineers was delivering ice and water. The two quickly made their way over to the appointed spot, anxious to take advantage of the supply. They were not the only ones desperate to receive the welcome delivery. They loaded the treasures into the back of the Tahoe ferrying it back to the restaurant. And for the first time in days, they enjoyed a cold beer, with ice cubes quickly melting in the paper cups.

Each evening the local holdouts gathered at the restaurant, each bringing some sort of non-perishable donation for the meal, a veritable smorgasbord of offerings. That evening it was complemented by cold drinks as well. All agreed they would not leave the sanctuary of their businesses.

"At least not until the weed gives out," Harry piped up, as he smiled towards Sarah. Sarah glanced at him quizzically. Was it possible he had changed?

At night the streets were still so quiet and empty you could hear paper rustling in the street. No people, no cars. It was a very different French Quarter with a strange dark tranquility.

CHAPTER 44

Thursday morning, Sarah and James decided to take a more in-depth look at what had happened to their city. Canal Street was lined with regional news vans. Some streets are still flooded but now drivable. Storefronts were gutted. Uptown, troops were on every corner. But the streets were empty of pedestrians. As they drove, certain areas had massive destruction and others were relatively clear, except for downed trees, empty of leaves. Piles of garbage littered the streets. Abandoned cars stood crashed in unusual formations, one upon another.

Although most areas near the river were dry, the ground still had a smell clinging to it. St. Charles was clear, but what was left was a toxic soup. The stench, even for James who was used to the smell of New Orleans, was beyond belief, like a mercury-laced swamp. In places where water still stood, millions of mosquito larvae floated.

They found a different kind of disaster in Chalmette. The storm had damaged the storage tanks of at one of the largest U.S. refineries. When the floodwaters rose to 18 feet, and the tank dislodged from its foundation, the oil had begun to leak. When the floodwater began to recede over a million gallons leaked into the adjacent residential area. The smell of oil would cling in the air for months.

Every third vehicle they drove past was military. Apache helicopter were flying patrols, low and slow about every five minutes. Soldiers were camped out on every dry corner. Signs were spray painted with "You Loot, We Shoot."

When Sarah and James reached the Garden District, they found a contingent of National Guard. The unit was going door to door seizing guns and forcing residents to leave. They quickly made their way out of there. Back in French Quarter they still had friends in the local police department that would support them.

Each night the storm survivors still met at the restaurant. Their discussion surrounded all the political name-calling going on in the media. Everyone seemed to be pointing fingers. They felt the Mayor was being made a scapegoat and agreed he was the one person who had actually done something. Somehow the storm had removed the division of politics from those who gathered together. Any disagreements they may have once had regarding Mayor Nagin had suddenly vanished. He had become their undisputed hero with his candid and honest remarks.

The group had become more and more ragged. What Sarah found surprising was that those that remained were a mixture of rich and poor, business owners and worker bees. In any other times, these groups would not have commingled in social situations. Because of Katrina, they were forced together and class was suddenly of no importance, equal at least in the eyes of the storm.

Two survivors stopped by to announce they had found jobs that day, happily making much more than they had before. They had been hired to clean the sidewalks.

And that weekend the head of FEMA finally resigned. The locals breathed a sigh of relief. Everyone was unanimous in their dislike of him. And finally, the news reported that the airport reopened, although with limited service. Life was returning.

CHAPTER 45

Sarah and James stock of supplies was dwindling. They decided to make a trip to Dallas. They finally reached her home in the suburb of Grapevine late Sunday evening. The two were exhausted. Sarah walked up to her front door and placed her key in the lock. Before she had it turned, her son had it opened. The two held each other tightly. She stepped back and looked into his face. He had changed in the months they had been apart. He was no longer her little boy.

She looked around at the home that had once been hers. It was no longer familiar. It now had a definite masculine atmosphere. The furniture was rearranged. This home now belonged to Terrence. The walls, once covered by floral landscapes, were swathed with hunting and fishing scenes.

The master bedroom now belonged to Terrence. At least he had not painted the pink and blue walls with its Southwestern border. For their visit, Terrence had moved his things so that they had a place to stay. Terrence had a typical male kitchen, cold cuts, cheese and beer. Together, they made sandwiches out the meager contents of the refrigerator. The drive had worn them out.

Sarah and James climbed the stairs to the bedroom, took a long hot shower and fell exhausted onto the bed. Holding each other under the crisp clean sheets, they made love, slowly caressing each other. The events of the past few weeks had brought them so much closer than they had ever been before.

"I love you so much", James whispered into her ear. "I couldn't have made it through the last few weeks without you. You are my life."

The next day, they packed up the Tahoe with everything required for the business and returned home with Agnes safely ensconced in the back seat. She had become used to her place in the vehicle and now happily jumped in the back as soon as the door was opened.

CHAPTER 46

The pair returned to the heat of the Quarter. It was still relatively empty, bar the few locals and military personnel. Still business was starting to return. With the supplies that they had brought back, they were able to bring a semblance of normality back to the restaurant.

And then the weather channels reported news of another disaster about to happen, Hurricane Rita. It appeared Nature's wrath was once again determined to ravage New Orleans. The mayor ordered another evacuation. Of course, there was no question in James or Sarah's mind of running from this storm.

Sarah's phone rang. It was Terrence. He and Steve, the owner of the company he worked for, had decided to rescue his boat from the Houston harbor. Houston also was under an evacuation order. As much as Sarah had no fear for herself, this was not the case when it concerned her children. She begged him not to go, but Terrence was just as hard-headed as she.

The trip to Houston took no time at all. The trip back was a completely different story. The roads were totally gridlocked, reminiscent of the flight from Katrina. It took Terrence and Steve forty-eight hours to drive the normal five hour distance. The media, swept away by the memory of Katrina, played on the emotions of the public. And the residents of Houston listened.

Terrence and Steve filled up the truck's tank as soon as they reached the marina. But in their haste, they did not fill up the boat. Pulling the weight of the boat, they were only averaging six miles to the gallon. Many were actually pushing their cars in order to conserve gas. At one point, the two friends even tried siphoning gas from the boat, but they couldn't get the hose to work properly.

Gas stations were either completely empty of gas or inundated with customers. The Wal-Mart gas station had cars lined up filling the entire parking lot all the way to the exit ramp. It was not until they were an hour outside Dallas that they found DOT crews delivering gas to the evacuees.

In order to go to the store, Terrence and Steve had to park almost two miles away and walk. What they found inside was a totally depleted store, no water and no ice, and lines and lines of customers. They grabbed some warm bottles of Dr. Pepper and what non-perishable food items that were still available and waited in the slowly moving queue.

As the two pulled the boat, they saw litter scattered along the roadways. Many people walked along the road, some pushing strollers in the 90 degree heat. The mood of the thousands of evacuees upon the roads was actually friendly, everyone in the same situation, calling and talking to the people in the other cars. Everyone had a story. It was a slow moving island of compassion. Steve and Terrence happily shared bottles of water with families walking beside them.

These refugees were eager to talk to someone, anyone, probably tired of talking to the same person they shared a vehicle with. If a car broke down, evacuees were quick to offer assistance. Although there was a sense of shock to the mass evacuation, there was no panic.

When the two finally arrived back in Dallas, they each retreated to their respective homes in order to get some well needed rest. Terrence was woken the next morning by a call from Steve's parents telling him of Steve's death. Hurricane Rita had taken another random victim. The long car ride had taken its toll on Steve's body, causing an arterial aneurism.

Terrence was devastated as he called Sarah to tell her the news. Sarah could not help but wonder how much more heartbreak this year would hold.

New Orleans did not sustain the brunt of Rita, but the strong winds did force the surge over the recently repaired levee. The Lower Ninth Ward was once again flooded. The only good thing that Rita brought was the rain to cool the oppressive heat. New Orleans had not seen rain since Katrina.

CHAPTER 47

On September 26th, Mayor Nagin officially reopened the French Quarter but it wasn't until September 28th that the area began to look alive. As darkness fell upon the streets, lamps and neon lights turned back on. The locals and relief workers roamed the area looking for action once more. But there were still few cars to be seen.

Along the streets, the trash bins were empty, although piles of stinking garbage still lined the streets. Their smell reeked in the heat of the day, but tended to diminish as the sun went down. There was still a curfew, but it was rarely enforced.

Luckily the restaurant used electric power. Those businesses that required gas would need to wait a few more days before that would be restored. The city wanted to make sure all the old buildings of the French Quarter were inspected before turning it back on and possibly causing another disaster.

The next few weeks would see the return of some of the residents of the town. As they returned the piles of garbage on the street corners would grow, as everyone attempted to clean out their homes. Thousands of refrigerators wrapped in tape lined the sidewalks like soldiers on parade.

The second week of October, an inspector from the FDA stopped by the restaurant. Since they had not left, they had been able to keep the place relatively clean on a daily basis. They did not have the massive mess to clean up that many of the other restaurateurs came back to. The inspector went through the refrigerator checking for bugs. He told them they were required to only use bottled soda and water. They were not allowed to make their own ice yet and had to prove it came from a reliable source. Happily, they grasped the issued permit.

By the second week in October, water service had been restored completely. Garbage pickup was on a regular basis. Once more, the restaurant began to serve on china with actual silverware. They were still short-staffed with only two of the wait staff having returned. Most of their staff had lost everything and had no place to return. Temporary housing was basically non-existent.

Sarah and James worked alongside the employees to help in the kitchen, bus the tables and wait on the guests. There was no shortage of customers. The restaurant was full with returning locals, construction workers, relief workers, FEMA, and military.

CHAPTER 48

The employees of the publishing company had started working again, although not yet having returned to New Orleans. Sue had made her way to her daughter's home in Chicago. And Sherry and Cathy found safety in Florida. Their laptops kept them in daily communication. Sarah would stretch herself between working the restaurant and her laptop. When the business was slow, she would make her way to James' office to work.

As October progressed, the sounds in the French Quarter began to be punctuated more and more by buzzing saws and hammers. Everyone was desperate to bring life back to the town. Even Café Du Monde reopened.

The third week of October saw the return of James' family. Sarah suddenly realized how the disaster had actually eased her relationship with James. With everything that had occurred since Katrina, they had relied entirely upon each other. There had been no one coming between them. The premonition of change sent shivers through her spine.

The parents returned to a home relatively unscathed by the disaster. There was a minor roof leak that had trickled down the walls, but nothing major. And their refrigerator would not be one left upon the sidewalk.

The father stopped by the restaurant and was happy to see that business was brisk. He commended James for his perseverance. His investment had been safeguarded, unlike that of many of his colleagues.

CHAPTER 49

By mid-November, the restaurant was fully staffed. Sarah and James decided to visit Hopedale.

Abandoned mud-encrusted cars still littered the highways. Mountains of garbage stood at the sides of roads. A refrigerator sat ominously upon the roof a house still standing. Everywhere, they saw massive destruction with little evidence of repair taking place.

The sky was dark and rain was drizzling. James stopped at the side of the road at a cemetery.

"This is the cemetery that is in the picture on my parent's wall," he stated.

Sarah had James stop so she could take a closer look. James remained in the car. She walked through the grounds, totally abandoned and destroyed. The old tree in the picture still stood forlorn. Many of the graves were torn apart and open, bodies nowhere to be seen. Inside one, Sarah saw a child's truck. She wondered where it had come from. Sarah shivered. Even the dead had not been safe from Katrina's wrath.

They passed a boat yard piled high with wreckage. Boats lay upon boats, barely recognizable.

"My father's boat is somewhere under all that rubble."

They were surprised to find the Hopedale retreat still

standing, although most of the outer walls were gone. There was nothing left inside, no furniture, no appliances. Just an empty shell of what had been.

CHAPTER 50

It would be a different Christmas that year. Many of the New Orleans aristocracy had still not returned. Many areas still had no electricity. If one strayed too far from the neighborhood at night, one would have a hard time finding their way back. Stoplights still did not work in the majority of the city. Stop signs stood at most intersections. Signs in windows like in an episode of Twilight Zone eerily announced sales that ended in September as if time had stopped.

There was no lack of humor in the spray painted signs found throughout the city. The people of New Orleans could still laugh at their situation. Letters to Santa, Entergy, and FEMA abounded. Christmas decorations were strewn over piles of garbage.

Mail delivery was still hit or miss, maybe two or three times a week, but only on 1st class mail.

Mail took about a week just to get to another address in New Orleans. Few Christmas cards would be sent or received that year.

James had never decorated his house for Christmas. But Sarah had been determined. She had elicited his help in placing lights around the house and upon the barren trees. She had even gotten his help in choosing a Christmas tree for the family room. Although she soon found out she would be the only one decorating it.

The Christmas Day meal was served at the newly reopened golf club. The lower level had sustained some water damage but the upstairs dining room was remarkably intact. Outside the window, stood the ancient oak tree, standing at attention, bare of leaves.

Together with the family, Sarah and James walked into the elegant hall. Everyone came up and shook hands. The gentry welcomed each other back. The room emanated with the sounds of a strange reunion, each one having been scattered to a different part of the country, each having a different story to tell. Throughout the meal one or another of the guests in the room would come to their table.

There was a definite shortage of wait staff. In fact, there was a definite shortage of workers throughout New Orleans, period. Much of the conversation revolved around finding help to clean or repair their homes. One of the women had even allowed her housekeeper to move into her Garden District home. The mother was horrified! You never know what those people might take.

Sarah remained a silent witness to the proceedings retreating once more to the island in her mind. By now, she was accustomed to the parent's attitude. She knew no questions would be asked of her. Her conversation was not required at this gathering.

She listened to a toast being given at the table next to them. Someone toasted Texas, thanking the state for accepting the undesirables. Maybe the gentry would get their city back.

Presents were exchanged and the couple retreated to the safety of their home, sparkling with the festive lights they had placed around the outside.

Back home alone once more they found the gifts for each other under the tree. James handed her three tiny boxes. "I love you more than you will ever know."

"And I love you more," was her reply. Inside the first box sat a pair of diamond earrings. Sarah immediately placed them in her ears. The second box held a golden heart-shaped bracelet. And the third held a diamond necklace.

James never stopped telling her of his love and she never got enough of hearing it.

Wrapping their arms around each other, they completed their second Christmas memory in the place they felt safest, the place no one could intrude, their bed.

CHAPTER 51

Sarah & James spent New Year's Eve with thousands of others listening to music by Arlo Guthrie and bidding good riddance to 2005. A jazz funeral procession marked the event.

Outside Jackson Square, a replica of a gumbo pot decorated with a picture of hot sauce slid down a pole. Fireworks burst into the sky. A new year was beginning.

Just after New Years, James came home from the restaurant, complaining of a pain in his shoulder and neck.

"I feel light headed like I will pass out, it's a weird feeling. I have no physical strength whatsoever and a headache that defies description."

His stomach hurt and all he wanted to do was go to bed. Sarah tried to get him to eat something but he had no appetite. He appeared to have a very bad case of the flu. But after a week, his condition had still not changed. Sarah begged him to see a doctor.

After a week and a half, James was barely making sense, floating in and out of consciousness. Sarah called the ambulance. She would not ask James for permission. While waiting for the ambulance, she called his parents. As they wheeled James into the emergency entrance, Sarah did not realize her life had forever changed.

James was immediately admitted. Sarah stood by his side, frightened to move for fear of what might happen. She held his hand tightly as he drifted between consciousness and unconsciousness. She wiped his brow when the sweat poured from his skin. Most of the time, he did not know she was there.

The tests went on for days and the final verdict was alcoholic hepatitis. Sarah had never considered James to have a drinking problem. They had their wine at night but during the day she never saw him drink, and when he did it usually wasn't to excess. So the diagnosis came as a shock.

This is when she found out that hiding his drinking from his parents had nothing to do with his DUI. James had had previous bouts with this disease in the past. When Sarah went home that evening she threw every bottle out. If James did make it through this, she was determined to be there to support him.

On the third day, James began to experience serious withdrawal symptoms. He pulled out the IV's and attempted to walk out of the hospital in his gown. When the guard tried to restrain him, the violence began. James began flailing at a male nurse, shattering his nose and breaking the hospital bed in the commotion. Eventually, he was forced in restraints. The hospital ordered a nurse to stay at his bedside full-time.

And then began the seizures. James would go into contortions, his face twisted in ghastly poses. His tongue would loll from his mouth and his hands would try pushing it back in his mouth. Sarah hated this time the most. It was then when she felt he might never come back. He might never be himself again.

James' parents would stop by every other day, but never stayed more than fifteen minutes. Sarah understood. It was hard to see him in this way. And most of the time he did not know they were there.

Sarah had James covered under her medical insurance. One day the mother questioned Sarah. Would her insurance cover an inpatient alcohol treatment program? Sarah really didn't believe this would be necessary but she looked into it for the mother. Although she found out that it would, Sarah prayed that she would not be forced to do this to James. She knew imprisonment of that kind would kill him. Sarah felt sure she would be able to free him from his need for alcohol.

When James did awaken, he became violent, in a voice unlike that Sarah had ever heard yelling at the nurses and once more pulling out the IV tubes. If Sarah was there, the anger would be directed at her. At these times she almost wished for the unconscious James.

"Get me out of here. If you loved me, you would get me released. Why are you doing this to me? You are in a conspiracy with my parents to keep me imprisoned here. Bring me my car, and I will drive myself home. I don't need you anymore."

Tears rolled down her face as the nurses looked on aghast.

Chapter 52

Carrie had returned to New Orleans and was doing a good job of managing the restaurant, but Sarah still felt a need to stop by each afternoon. The staff was eager to help keep the place running. It was a job and now that the gentry were back, the money was pretty good.

The end of the second week, James began to regain his sanity. Sarah would bring Agnes with her to the hospital and wheel James outside. This seemed to help his emotions.

After three weeks of trying to hold the business, her job, James and Agnes together, Sarah was exhausted. She would have loved to have either of his parents to offer to help with the restaurant. After all, in reality it did belong to them.

And finally the day came when he was released. Sarah ignored the mother's request. She lovingly brought him home and helped him into bed. The last three weeks had left him weak, too weak to do any more than make it to the bathroom and back. Slowly he began to eat again. And slowly he became the man she once knew. She once again lay in his arms and gently made love to his ravaged body.

He had gotten clean of the alcohol in his system and did not seem to miss it. After work they walked Agnes down by the water and let her swim happily content. Life seemed to return, calmer than before. They had their little family.

CHAPTER 53

Sarah carefully made plans for James' birthday. She made hotel reservations and found a kennel for Agnes. She hoped a weekend away from the stresses of the last few months would help them return to the passion they had once had. On the Friday afternoon before the planned retreat James went to visit his parents.

When he returned, his eyes were dead. He dropped sluggishly upon the couch. Sarah placed herself down beside him, protectively placing her arms around him.

"Whatever is wrong, my love. What is it? Please speak to me."

A premonition of intense terror overtook her. This involved her.

"I don't know how to tell you this," he started. "We need to break up."

"I don't understand. What is going on?" she blurted as the tears began to fall.

"We can't be together," he replied with tears in his eyes. "I love you. I will always love you, but we can't be together." Agnes looked on in silence, no longer wagging her tail.

Sarah, dumbfounded, slowly picked up her purse, mascara running down her face and walked out the door without uttering another word. She knew this had something to do with his parents and she had no control.

She got in her car and drove to the hotel she had booked in the Quarter. She had no idea what to do or where to go. She couldn't think. She was in a state of shock. She tossed and turned throughout the night, trying to make sense of what had happened.

Going to her office on Monday, she placed their picture taken at the wedding inside her desk. She tried to get on with her work, wanting to talk to someone but not knowing how. She was utterly lost.

CHAPTER 54

James' e-mails began immediately.

"Darling:

This has been the hardest thing I have ever had to do. I miss you so much. I may have been depressed before I met you but nothing like this. I do love you with all my heart. But we just can't be together. It can never work between us. There are too many things against us. I hate society.

Love forever, James."

Sarah did not answer. And thus the e-mails continued, every few hours, begging her to speak to him. Sarah remained silent.

She knew she had to get some clothes for work, so she went over to the house when she knew he would not be home. Agnes lay sleeping by the door but jumped up energetically when Sarah walked in. The lab sauntered against her leg, not understanding what was going on. Sarah reached down and clasped her tightly. She snuggled in her embrace. Agnes followed Sarah through the house as she picked up the few things she needed, at least until she made some decisions.

And then she walked into the kitchen to retrieve the cell phone she had left there. Upon the counter sat a large half empty bottle of whiskey, something she had never seen James drink before. Inside the refrigerator stood a bottle of white wine, something else she had never seen him drink. She was horrified. And she knew there was absolutely nothing she could do.

Sarah walked towards the door. Agnes sauntered close to Sarah, as if attached to her leg. The dog looked up into her eyes, silently pleading with her to stay. Sarah knelt down in the quiet hallway, tears streaming, knowing she was losing her too. Agnes, who rarely showed affection to anyone, kissed Sarah's face repeatedly. Sarah wrapped her arms around the dog, then stood up and closed the door softly behind her.

Sarah confided in no one, not her children, not her co-workers. She had been warned about this, but had chosen to ignore their fears. She foolishly had believed love could conquer all.

CHAPTER 55

By the end of the week, James could take her silence no longer. Not knowing where she was staying or anything about her, he drove to her office and met her as she came out of the door.

"Please talk to me. I need to talk to you. I miss you so much. All I do is cry. I miss having you come in the door at night. I miss just speaking of how our days went. I hate the way I feel. I feel so weak. I cannot satisfy everyone and it makes me want to lose my mind. Please let's just go somewhere and talk." He wrapped his arms around her. "I miss holding you. I need you."

Sarah looked into his eyes and melted. He followed her to the hotel. And the passion that had diminished since his illness flared up once more. He held her tight throughout the night, waking up sporadically to continue the lovemaking. In the morning, they ordered breakfast to the room, hoping to hide from the world.

"I have never loved anyone like I love you. The last two years have been the best of my life. I lived alone for so long before I met you, I guess I got used to not having anyone around on a daily basis like that. And now I am alone again. I feel so lost without you. I can't stand to see you cry and know what I have done to you. You have every reason to hate me for this," James spoke quietly.

"I could never hate you. You have been the greatest love of my life. I have never felt such passion before. I wish I knew what to say. I truly love you and nothing has or will change on my part. When I spoke of loving you forever, my words were real. That is not going to change because we are not together. I am sure eventually the pain will diminish, although at this point I can't see how. I hate being alone. I hate having no one to talk to. I miss just having someone to tell about the things that go on at work. I miss hearing about your day. I miss having someone hold me. I guess I just wish I had someone to talk to. I know we both need to be married and that can never be to each other. All I can do is love you enough to let you go," Sarah replied.

They spent the day hiding inside the room, talking of the island where they might go to hide from the world. The weekend ended too soon.

CHAPTER 56

But the e-mails and phone calls continued. And the surreptitious visits to her hotel room. As the weeks dragged on Sarah looked forward to the nightly visits, knowing that one day they would have to end. They spoke of a fantasy world where no one could intrude, but knew in their hearts that could never be.

James spoke of his pain and the ache in his heart. "I cannot function. All I want to do is to find something to take my mind off this turmoil inside my head. In all honesty, I just want to get drunk and go to sleep but I know it will accomplish absolutely nothing…it does make the pain go away some though. I really hate society. Where is that deserted island????? "

Sarah shivered, knowing the truth behind the words. "I don't want you to do anything to hurt yourself. You mean too much to me. I will do whatever it takes to make you feel better."

They spoke of their "moments" together, moments that no one could take away. But they spoke to no one else. The parents felt sure it had ended, as did his employees. And Sarah spoke to no one, not her family or her co-workers. James knew this was tearing her apart.

"Why not talk to Sue?" he encouraged. "It's hard keeping all this from others. You are always the strong one, maybe it's time to get back a little of the support you've been giving. I am here for you, but I am sure it is not quite the same. I am getting sick of work. I just want to go home and hide from the world, though I know it won't do any good. I am particularly depressed today. I miss you so much."

Sarah countered, "Keeping this from everyone is the only way I can get through this. One day when I am really strong, I will face the world. Right now it is too hard. They have to know that I will be alright. A few months from now I will be able to say we broke up "x" months ago and no one will feel the need to save me. I can't stand the thought of anyone thinking negative of you. So for now you are the only one I want to talk to. I miss you so much. It's like I have a lump in my throat but it is in my heart."

"A lump huh? It's like cancer for me! I am the one who has given in. I don't know what to do. As I have said before the guilt is killing me. You are the last person in the world I want to hurt but I am afraid of hurting you more by letting this go on. I am having a difficult time. It is like I have to choose between you and my family...and I don't want to make a decision. It is awful to be in this position. Keeping it secret has helped me a lot but the "moments" will come to an end and that thought alone makes me want to cry. Even if your family hates me for what I have done to you, you will know, I do LOVE you. Things would be easier if you "hated me for what I have done, but even though it would be easier I like it much better this way (sharing our moments). I'm a glutton for punishment. If I'm smart I'll stay single forever...Agnes can inherit the restaurant and you can run it for her...lol. She won't mind if you take the profits."

CHAPTER 57

The turmoil inside kept her from focusing on work. Even her co-workers could see there was something wrong. But no one could put their finger on it. She was no longer the smiling happy-go-lucky person they had come to know. Finally Sue questioned her. And the story came out as tears rolled down Sarah's face.

Sue asked what she was planning to do. Sarah had considered moving back to Dallas, but Sue was adamant that she stay. At this point, Sarah didn't know where to go. She was in a total state of confusion.

She told James that night of her conversation. "If I make a decision at this point, I could just be making another mistake. Right now I am just making decisions a day at a time."

He looked shocked. "I totally understand the day to day decision-making. But I kind of thought you liked your new job so much you would stay in New Orleans."

"I do love my job. In fact I have never had a job I like more. But here I have no one—no friends, no family. I have never been this isolated in my life. I need a support system. We never really needed anyone when we lived together. We always had each other."

"A great job is hard to find. You were and are so energetic with all the aspects of your job. I feel guilty about even expressing an opinion. I broke your heart and mine too." James was not ready to lose her completely.

Throughout the workdays, his short e-mail messages would appear. And James waited impatiently for her replies. Even on days when there was not much to say, it was just nice to hear from her.

"I love our moments," she'd write.

"I have had tears in my eyes all morning. It hurts me to see you and know I can't have you forever. I don't need to cry anymore if possible. Would you mind company tonight?" he begged.

"I can feel your arms around me…feels so good. I can't wait to walk through your door this evening. Why can't I get you out of my mind for just a second? The things you do to me! Love, James."

"I don't want to be out of your mind. I talk to you all the time, even when you are not with me. I guess you are just hearing my thoughts. Love, Sarah."

"LOL…I like that way of looking at my insanity." He quickly replied. "So when are we leaving for that deserted island again?"

"Is now too soon? Sarah replied.

"Whenever, we just have to figure out how to keep it secret! The world is truly a cruel place!" James responded.

And Sarah succumbed to their illicit life. Each night was spent in a passionate embrace. She knew as long as he was with her, he was not drinking. And as much as they had spoken to each other when they lived together, they spoke even more now. But they both knew they were only postponing the inevitable.

"Would you like to come over tonight" she e-mailed.

"I would love to have your company tonight. The thought of

you melting into my arms is very appealing. How late do you think you will be?"

"With that kind of invitation, I would like to leave right now," she replied. "But I guess I should stay till five. Do you want me to pick up something to eat?"

"That would be great but I am not sure what I want besides you."

The parents had gotten what they wanted, at least they thought so. She knew the parents still spoke to him questioning why she had not moved back to Dallas. They did not want her anywhere near him, infecting him once again.

"I just got off the phone with my Dad. It makes me very uneasy to basically lie to him about what's been going on recently between us. I hate this feeling," James called to complain one day.

"Does he have any idea how you have been feeling?" Sarah said softly, well aware that the inevitable was bound to come, well aware that lying was a way of life in New Orleans.

"He knows it's very hard for me. I miss you so much, Sarah. I can't help but to think that you won't be in my life daily in the future. It really hurts me as I'm sure it does you as well. It is hard to live with just the moments but I treasure each one. As I've said before, if I ever walk down the aisle you can be assured that I will thinking of you and smile and wonder if I let the best thing I ever had slip away. I love you so much."

"I know we are letting the best thing either of us will ever have slip away. I don't think I ever believed in soul mates before, but I do now. We think too much alike to be anything else. I can't tell you how many times I have said something to Sue that you later repeated to me almost exactly. Like walking down the aisle. I miss you so much. But I treasure whatever time we might have left."

"You are so understanding. I will always treasure the time we had together. Having someone as special as you is more than I could ask for. Sometimes I hate my family. They probably think that I'll get over it" or "it will be for the best"…Maybe yes and maybe no, but certainly not quickly or any time in the near future will I feel better about it. I hate to think I missed my soul mate," James continued.

"For now let's live for today. The future is not anything I want to contemplate. I just want to ignore their intrusions. I just worry they might attempt another intervention. You probably shouldn't stand up for me when they start talking badly about me. They might realize you still care and that will increase their fervor."

"Yes I agree we have to live for the moment. Hiding this is not what I envisioned. I can't believe (or don't want to) that my happiness is not their major concern. It hurts. Don't worry, I won't mention you. I've already expressed the pain and anguish I am going through. They don't say much about it. I can't however let them speak negatively about you because you have done nothing wrong. I'll just defend you and let them think we are not together. At least it might let them know how much I do care for you no matter what their opinion may be. I am always thinking of you."

The James started speaking of selling the house. "It holds so many memories of you. Even the paint you chose for the walls reminds me of you. I can't stand living here anymore. What if we bought condos in the same building? Then I could see you whenever I wanted. And my parents wouldn't have to know you live there too."

James even went so far as to look at condos that had two available units. Sarah knew this was not the answer. It was just a dream. Just like their island.

CHAPTER 58

For a while the visits helped them both. But the inevitability of the situation caused them to bounce between happiness and depression. Some mornings they both left with tears in their eyes, not knowing which way to turn.

"I love my time with you when we are just being us," Sarah e-mailed. "I can focus on my work or whatever I am doing when my mind is not running a mile a minute on the problems between us. I read into everything you say and everything hurts."

"Please don't read into what I say too deeply. I don't want you to hurt. Make me hurt...I would much prefer that. Please don't let your work suffer. It sounds awful, but if your work suffers, I will feel worse than I already do. You will be successful in whatever you do. I know that in my heart. No one can keep you down. You are too strong for that. I never want to go through that Friday again. I love being close to you but it scares the hell out of me. I am trying to do the impossible, make everyone happy. In the mean time I end up miserable. You have the most genuine love for me than anyone and that really freaks me out. No one except you knows just how I feel. I'll love you forever," came his reply.

Sarah regularly continued to review the restaurant accounting. She knew the regular accountant had a tendency to make mistakes, and it was only under Sarah's watchful eye that she could make sure this did not occur.

"I want things to go good for the restaurant," she told him. "I still feel a part of it."

"You are a part of the business. Everywhere I look I see how much you have done and how much you have helped me. You have no idea how much I appreciate you."

The stress of the situation was getting to Sarah. One morning she even missed a meeting. This was not in character for her. She was usually so organized. She e-mailed to tell him, although no one had complained of her absence.

He was sure she would not get in trouble, which of course, she didn't. "They need you too much there to get upset with you. I can relate."

Another time she almost ran out of gas, in not one of the best areas of town. James was horrified. He began to envision accidents any time he did not hear from her. James became frantic when she did not reply to an e-mail immediately. Any news reports of accidents on the road would have him immediately calling or e-mailing Sarah to assure himself that she was okay.

Now that he no longer possessed her, his possessiveness grew. He needed to know where she was every minute.

"Are you there? I am just making sure you are okay." More than once that message would be displayed on her computer by the time she arrived in the office.

As the weeks passed, the rambling e-mails began to display their mutual lack of interest in work.

"I cannot function today. All I want to do is find something to take my mind off this turmoil inside of my head. I really hate society…where is that deserted island??? My thoughts of you are always good. I am just not feeling that good about myself.

You mean the world to me. I wish love could conquer all but it can't. Only moments…are what we have. I love you."

"I am having difficulty concentrating too," Sarah returned.

"I am so sorry darling. I don't want things to be difficult for you. I guess I want us both to be happy in a situation which is totally miserable. It's a catch 22 no matter how I think of it. I am trying to make everything the best I can for all involved but nothing seems to work. I would rather have everything blamed on me and put on my shoulders so no one else has to suffer. I miss you so much!"

Chapter 59

The parents continued to ask him over. He got a pit in his stomach each time he was summoned. He hated these interactions. But he knew he needed to, if only for the business. They would question him as why Sarah was still in the hotel. They wanted her to disappear permanently. He came back from these meetings totally drained.

"I am feeling so alone," he complained to Sarah one evening after a particularly difficult visit.

"I don't want you to feel alone. I am here to talk to. You can have me anytime you want. All you have to do is ask. And I'm asking for nothing in return (just breakfast, lunch, dessert, snack, dinner, afternoon delight, etc.)," Sarah stated, trying to interject some of the humor from their earlier days. "And as long as your parents and friends don't know, you're keeping them happy too. And you are really not alone right now. I am still here."

"I don't want to feel alone, but the fact remains that I am! You can have me for any snack or meal you want! It just hits me hard at times that forever can't happen with us. I just need a hug…It just seems like I have good days and bad ones. Today is not a good one. I often wonder whether my parents have any idea what I am going through. Not everyone can have a picture perfect life."

"You really don't want to ask me questions about your parents. Or my opinion." Sarah knew this was a dangerous subject.

"Oh yes I do want your opinion. I think I will agree with you more than you think I will."

She realized the inevitable was only a matter of time.

Sarah knew the loneliness of the house was getting to him. The loneliness of the hotel was definitely getting to her. The depression was evident. His visits were coming less often. James would find himself going home after work, barely acknowledging Agnes, and sit down blankly in front of the television. He didn't have the energy to even concern himself with what was on.

The house did not just return to its pre-Sarah state, but actually much worse. A black mildew grew around the inside of the tub and the toilets. Roaches began to crawl across the counters. It may have survived Katrina intact, but it would not survive this. Dishes piled in the sink, until all he used was paper and plastic utensils. Agnes began to display similar symptoms, relieving herself upon the floors. James had no energy or desire to clean it. For what?

And, outside of Sarah's watchful eye, the drinking increased.

Sarah knew he wasn't eating properly, if at all. He was certainly losing weight, requiring a belt just to keep his pants up. She began to stop off and pick up takeout meals on night she knew he would be coming over.

CHAPTER 60

As James' depression advanced, his lethargy grew. His employees saw no reason to expend energy on the business when the owner himself did not. The level of service began to drop as did the customers. He would leave work early and go to his empty house, pour himself a drink, and lay upon the couch. By the time Sarah would get off work, he would be in too much of a stupor to see her.

When he did show any interest in the business, it was usually just to blow up at the employees or whoever was nearest at the moment. His temper would flare at the slightest provocation. All the pent up anger he felt towards his parents would be released tenfold upon the unsuspecting workers. Even Carrie, who had been with the business since the beginning, could not escape his wrath. Thinking she might now have a chance with him, she had begun dieting, hoping he might finally notice. But instead his wrath grew.

"Work is so aggravating today…Carrie just doesn't seem to get it! It's things that are common sense…She takes it as a tremendous insult when I say that something is common sense…But I can't help the fact that it is common sense! There are just some things she does not think are a big deal, like keeping things running efficiently. She doesn't seem to realize that's her job! I know you think I am hard on her but this is ridiculous," he ranted.

Sarah tried to assuage his rage, but to no avail. And then one day, Carrie showed up no more. The poor girl finally realized any dreams she had of getting James to love her were gone.

None of his workers would escape his tirades.

"People are making way too many mistakes today. I feel like if I am not here, the world goes to hell! It's the dumb look of 'I didn't know' even though it's been done the same way thousands of times before which really pisses me off. If they don't care they should find another job. And they think they deserve minimum wage increase…for what, stupidity…I need to hire some monkeys and feed them bananas! It's cheaper and they'd probably be more accurate with the right amount of bananas…and their cheap!" he raged.

Even his customers became subject to his rage. "The woman was so aggravating. I just wanted to tell her to go to Antoine's and leave me alone. Maybe it's just my mood these days."

He was complaining again of the pain in his back and in his stomach. Sarah advised him to go back to the doctor, but he would not go. Almost daily he was gripped by bouts of nausea. His appetite diminished to nothing.

CHAPTER 61

Good Friday Sarah went in to work to find no e-mails. This was not like James. He wrote each morning even when there was nothing to say. She sent an e-mail, she sent a text message, and when he didn't respond, she phoned his cell. No answer. Although she never called work, she began to get so worried, she decided she had to. They had not seen him. And he had not called. Fear gripped her.

Sarah grabbed her purse and raced over to his house. The Tahoe still stood in the driveway. She knocked but there was no answer. Digging deep into her purse, she found the key she had not used in so long. Opening the lock with trembling fingers, she rushed inside. James lay on the couch, barely conscious. Alice stood, her tongue licking his face. Sarah tried to talk to him, but he was delirious. She immediately called 911 and cried for an ambulance. He was rushed to the hospital and admitted once more. Once again, she had to call his parents.

When the parents got to the hospital, there was rage in their eyes. They had thought this affair was over. What was she doing here with him? If James was back in the hospital, it must be her fault. Why did she not just go away?

This time the doctors knew what to test for. There was no question what was wrong. The hepatitis was back.

CHAPTER 62

There was no one to look after Agnes so Sarah moved her things back into James' house, without the parents' permission. She went to work cleaning the disaster that had become his home. Once more, she disposed of the bottles of alcohol that lined the counter. Agnes remained close by her side, frightened Sarah might disappear again.

James drifted in and out of consciousness throughout the next few weeks. When he was aware of his surroundings, his verbal communications made no sense. And these periods of understanding began to come less and less. As the weeks turned into months, James no longer seemed to identify with anyone. It started with the recognition of his parents. And it ended with Sarah.

His once-bright green eyes were clouded, looking out but without any recognition. No smile formed upon his lips. No words were uttered from his mouth. The doctors pulled Sarah aside, stating there was no more that could be done. He would need to be sent to a nursing home.

Sarah was adamant. She wanted to bring him home and look after him. She was determined to hold on to her decaying love at all costs. But she would not be allowed to have a say in this matter. She was not related to James. His parents alone held the power to make decisions for him. And the decision was made. An ambulance arrived to ferry the body of what once had been James to a nursing home about an hour from New Orleans.

The very next weekend, the parents called and told her she needed to remove the things she still had at his house. She needed to move. She packed the things she had brought and looked around at their once familiar home. She went to the bathroom and opened the tiny jewelry boxes which held all the gifts James had given her. She placed the heart shaped bracelet across her wrist and the tears began to fall. She had stayed strong throughout the whole ordeal. But she could hold it back no longer. She looked in the mirror. Her black eyes were bloodshot. The diamond necklace James had given her still sparkled against her skin, but her clouded eyes could not see it. And then there was Agnes. She picked up her cell phone and asked permission to keep her. They had no problem with that. She needed at least something that belonged to James.

Sarah moved what little she had to Sherry's house. Sherry's husband, Jim, graciously, accepted her into their home. The spare bedroom was cleared out for her. Sherry and Jim had a dog of their own and did not mind Agnes. Sarah wasn't ready to make any decisions with her life. She could always go back to her job in Dallas and her home. But this was where the love of her life still lived, even if he no longer knew who she was.

CHAPTER 63

Katrina had ravaged New Orleans, and now that the gentry were back, prejudice had destroyed their love. As Katrina had swooped down upon this town, engulfing it, turning everything upside down, so had this inbred hatred turned two lives upside down. And nothing would ever be the same again. There was no turning back. There would be restoration for New Orleans but there would be none for their love.

On the weekend, Sarah made her way to the nursing home. James was thrashing, throwing off his covers, trying to escape the ties that bound him to the bed. The sounds coming from his mouth were no longer human. Sarah held his hand gently in hers. For a second, she thought she saw a sign of recognition, but then realized it was probably only wishful thinking. For hours she sat at his side as his body was thrown into contortions. The shifts of nurses came and went. Sarah stayed.

As night fell, Sarah's despair at her helplessness took over. She gently closed the door to his room, went over to his side, and slipped off the clothes she had on. She climbed into the bed and held his body next to her skin. The thrashing subsided as he lay silent in her arms. He still showed no signs of recognition, but at least he was peaceful. Sarah moved her hands over his body gently caressing him. And he drifted off to sleep. And then so did Sarah.

The morning nurse found them wrapped in each other's arms, both peacefully at rest. She gently wakened Sarah and warned her that his parents had just arrived. She needed to leave. Sarah quickly dressed and was slipping out the door when they came in.

The anger was apparent in their eyes. They were furious that she was there invading their territory. But they spoke no words to her. Sarah slowly walked down the hall and out the doors.

The following weekend Sarah again went visit James. She walked past the nurse's desk and into his room. The contortions and thrashing were back. A nurse came up behind her.

"You are not allowed in here anymore. His parents are paying for this facility and we must honor their wishes."

Sarah stepped back in horror. This could not be happening. They could not be taking him away from her again. She could not hurt them now.

She turned around and walked back outside. Tears streamed from her face as she drove back to New Orleans. When she got to Sherry and Jim's house, she called the parents to beg them to let her see him. The housekeeper answered. They were not there and would not be back for 3 months. They had sold the restaurant and had left on a world cruise.

CHAPTER 64

Sarah knew she had an ally with one of the night nurses, so on the weekends she would arrive late at night to calm James' with her body. And before daybreak, she would slip back out. She was back to their surreptitious visits, even though James was unaware of her existence. At least she still knew him.

On one of these visits, a doctor noticed her slipping into the room. He questioned the nurse as to who she was and what she was doing there. The nurse quietly explained the circumstances. He was shocked at her devotion. Most of these patients received visits from no one. And this patient who recognized no one had a regular guest.

The doctor began to schedule his weekend visits to the home late at night to catch a glimpse of this secret visitor. He was enchanted by her, both by her looks and her compassion. But it would be months before he had the nerve to confront her. When he did, he looked into her black eyes and knew she was someone he wanted for his own. He was willing to take the chance that someday she would feel the same for him.

Their romance started slowly, meeting over coffee, his blue eyes gazing into hers. His children and family fell in love with her immediately. And her family fell in love with him. It would be a year before he had the nerve to ask her to marry him.

He knew she still visited James, but he realized that part of her life was something he could not take from her. He knew somehow she offered peace to this poor man who had no other visitors.

EPILOGUE

The moment suddenly vanished and Sarah was back in the present, looking into the blue eyes of the man who was giving her his name. She glanced behind her in the front pews of the tiny church. There was his family and her family sitting together as one, smiles upon their faces. She was where she belonged. She turned back to look at him and said "I do." The moment was over and a new moment was beginning.

Katrina was over. An island was no longer needed. A new life was about to be created.